LAURIE BENSON

Mrs. Sommersby's Second Chance

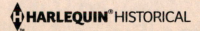

Laurie Benson is an award-winning Regency romance author whose book *An Unexpected Countess* featured Harlequin's 2017 Hero of the Year, as voted by readers. She began her writing career as an advertising copywriter. When she isn't at her laptop avoiding laundry, Laurie can be found browsing antiques shops and going on long hikes with her husband and two sons. Learn more about Laurie by visiting her website at lauriebenson.net. You can also find her on Twitter and Facebook.

Books by Laurie Benson

Harlequin Historical

The Sommersby Brides

One Week to Wed
Convenient Christmas Brides
"One Night Under the Mistletoe"
His Three-Day Duchess
Mrs. Sommersby's Second Chance

Secret Lives of the Ton

An Unsuitable Duchess
An Uncommon Duke
An Unexpected Countess

Visit the Author Profile page at Harlequin.com.

Chapter One

Bath, England—1820

It wasn't as if a small sip of water was capable of changing one's life. In all the years Clara Sommersby had stood in the Pump Room to have her daily drink, she had never witnessed anyone perform such an intense inspection of a glass of the spa's mineral water.

She had seen the tall blond-haired gentleman accept the empty glass from the attendant and approach the fountain out of the corner of her eye. Many people entered Bath each day to stay for an extended amount of time to take advantage of the waters in hopes of alleviating their ailments. There were also those who came to the fashionable town to experience the noted assemblies and various entertainments. She would firmly place this gentleman in the latter category.

While Clara normally took note of newly arrived visitors, this morning she awoke with a soreness in her lower back and had only been thinking of a long soak in the thermal baths to hopefully relieve her discomfort—until she saw this man swirl the water in his glass and sniff it as one would do while studying a glass of wine.

For all she knew, he might be staying at The Fountain Head Hotel. It was in her best interest to create a favourable impression of the town.

'I'm sure whatever it is that ails you, you will find relief here.'

He seemed surprised she assumed he was here because he needed help. 'I have no ailments that I'm aware of.'

Two finely dressed young ladies approached Clara's side and dipped their glasses into the streams of water, while trying to catch the gentleman's eye. Instead of offering them some form of encouragement, he reverted his attention back to studying his glass until they walked away, giggling and whispering as they went.

When they were alone once again, he eyed Clara across the fountain. 'And you, madam, certainly you are much too young to suffer from any of those ills you spoke of. What brings you to the spa?'

'I am not as young as you might think.'

'Come now, you're not any older than I am.'

Ah, so he was one of those gentlemen who liked to flatter women. She had run across many of them in her life. By her estimation he appeared to be in his midthirties, which was ten years younger than she was.

'Perhaps this fountain also holds the key to a youthful appearance,' she teased. 'I have been drinking from it for many years now.'

A small smile tugged at the corner of his lips and softened the hard angles of his features. 'Then the waters here are far better than those in Tunbridge Wells. I don't believe they'd dare to make that claim.' Suddenly, his features hardened once more as he appeared to study her. 'Perhaps you are one of those charlatans, like the men and women selling miracle elixirs out-

gentlemen—to keep returning to her establishment. The Hotel meant everything to her. It was her security for financial independence and its success was something she took great pride in.

'I'm trying to determine if you're a good actress or if indeed the water is not as bad as I've been imagining.'

Had anyone ever been this hesitant to try the water? His procrastination was rather amusing. 'There is only one way to find out.' She cocked her head to the side and gave him an encouraging nod.

It wasn't as if a small sip of water was going to change his life. It might keep him close to a chamber pot for a good part of the day, but that would pass. At least that's what Mr William Lane silently hoped was the case as he had accepted a glass from the attendant and walked over to the King's Spring fountain in the Pump Room in Bath. Water cascaded down from spigots at the top of a pale stone urn into the open mouths of painted fish below. It was a clever feat of design engineering to get the water to fall just so and Lane took note of it, along with the other observations he was making of the interior design of this public space.

He dipped his glass into one of the streams of water, breaking the flow and filling his glass with the warm liquid. He had yet to try the thermal water his workmen had uncovered underneath the building he had just purchased, but thought it wise to try the popular water in the King's Spring first so he would have something to compare it to. If he offered it to customers to drink and reap the reputed benefits, he knew people would expect it to taste the same.

Lane raised the glass slowly to his lips and gave it a sniff as if he was sampling a fine bottle of wine. The

per glass for the first few months it would be a way to entice patrons of this spa to the one he might build. He just needed to find a way to convince his partner that this was a lucrative investment.

'Drink up, my boy,' the balding man wearing spectacles called to him from the other side of the fountain. 'You will experience none of the benefits of the water if you simply hold it in your glass. The water needs to be hot to be at its most effective.'

Lane must have been eyeing the room longer than he realised for it to be remarked upon. Out of the corner of his eye, he could see the woman beside him take another sip from her glass.

'You find the water beneficial? I admit I've been hesitant in trying it.'

There was a faint tsking sound from the woman next to him and he could see her shake her head ever so slightly, right before the white-haired, portly gentleman answered him.

'Nonsense,' he replied, his runny pale blue eyes narrowing on Lane under his thick, bushy, white eyebrows. 'There is no reason to hesitate. This water will not kill you. It cures rheums, palsies, lethargies, apoplexy, cramps, forgetfulness, trembling of any manner, aches and swelling of the joints, and even deafness.'

'What was that?' the other man asked him.

'I said the water has been known to cure those who are deaf.'

The balding man shook his head. 'Well, it helps with ailments, does nothing for theft.'

'Deaf. I said it cures deafness,' the other man said louder.

'Oh, rightly so. I've been coming here every day for a year and drink three pints a day. Works wonders.'

while graceful, were spry. Perhaps she just enjoyed the feel of the hot water.

An image of the woman with her dark hair piled high on her head, soaking in the large stone bath as her skin glistening with the steam of the water, filled his mind. Did they bathe naked here in the spa? He imagined the smooth swell of her breasts submerged partially in the hot water and he swallowed hard, thinking about swimming up to her and licking the water from her soft skin. The pool of water he spied below was large, which would leave them with plenty of room to explore one another below the surface of the water or on one of the stone steps leading down into the bath. In his mind, he pictured them in there, after the spa had been closed up for the night. Those musings quickly ended with the words of the white-haired gentleman across from him.

'Blockage of the bowels.'

Lane blinked a few times, bringing the room back into focus as he felt his eyebrows rise. 'Pardon?'

There was a soft sputter of laughter from the woman he had been daydreaming about, before she covered her mouth with her gloved hand and pretended to cough.

'I said blockage of the bowels,' the man repeated a bit louder. 'It also cures blockage of the bowels. Is that why you're here? Or is it for the women? Many fine women here in this town.' The man eyed the Duchess on his right.

She raised her chin and arched a very regal-looking brow at the man who appeared older than her advanced age. Her expression had the effect she intended since he moved a few steps away from her and shifted his attention back to Lane. None of them had been introduced to him and yet they all seemed perfectly content to speak with him about the advantages of taking the water here. Was all of Bath like this or was it some-

Lane glanced at the woman beside him before addressing the Duchess. 'I've never given it any thought.'

'But surely you have preferences in the women you spend your time with.'

He was being watched too closely by the four people in this group. Why couldn't they still be discussing the benefits of the water? He downed the contents of the glass in his hand, forgetting it was the spa water. If only he could wipe his tongue on his sleeve to alleviate the coppery taste in his mouth. He had learned not to care what other people thought of him a long time ago, but he found he didn't want the woman beside him to think him lily-livered. It was not the impression he wanted to leave her with.

'An interesting way to avoid answering a question,' she commented. Her brown eyes held that now-familiar hint of amusement under her arched brow.

Lane had come here to gather information. That was all. How had he become a source of entertainment for her?

'Well?' she asked.

'I've never given much thought to the type of women I prefer.'

'I meant the water.'

'Oh.' There were no mineral deposits at the bottom of his glass. And, thankfully, no strands of hair. 'It was not what I expected.'

'You'll grow accustomed to it. You may find you prefer it when it's hot. Since you held it for so long, I'm certain it would have cooled off in your glass.'

He hadn't planned to come back to this spa to find out. One visit should be enough to see what features he might want to recreate in his. With enough information, he was certain he could convince his partner that

Chapter Two

The sun had finally come out from behind the clouds and was shining high above the garden that was behind Clara's house in the Royal Crescent. This lovely garden, with a large variety of colourful roses, was one of her favourite places to spend her time in the warmer weather. On this spring day, she was enjoying the company of Eleanor, the Dowager Duchess of Lyonsdale, who she had run into at the Pump Room the day before. They were seated across from one another at the small round table that was set out on the gravel circle at the very centre of the garden.

The women had become friendly five years ago when they had worked together on a committee raising funds for the Foundling Hospital in London. Days were never dull when Eleanor was around and, for that, Clara was grateful.

'You always do have the most exceptional tea,' the Dowager commented, lowering her fine porcelain cup into its saucer and placing it on the table.

'Thank you. I've blended a few special types of oolong for this pot.'

The weight of the head of Clara's Cavalier King Charles spaniel rested on her foot while Humphrey

ton for two years after their parents passed, but we found it was better for her to stay with me in Bath than with them.'

'I suppose living with one's older sister can be trying at times and Skeffington certainly did not have the nicest disposition.' The Dowager broke off another piece of her biscuit. 'At the time that the two of you left London, I thought it might've had something to do with the Duke of Winterbourne's youngest brother, Lord Montague. But Juliet and Monty are married now, so perhaps that assumption was incorrect.' Her gaze held Clara's for a few breaths longer than necessary before she placed the piece of biscuit in her mouth.

'I don't know what you mean.'

How was it that this woman always seemed to know things that should have been a secret? Clara's niece Juliet had suffered terrible heartbreak at the hands of Lord Montague Pearce when her guardian refused to allow them to marry. At the time, Clara had taken Juliet out of London to spare her the pain of having to see Monty. The experience had created a close bond between the two women and while Clara had been so delighted that Juliet had finally found her happiness with Monty years later, Juliet's absence had left a hole in her heart.

The Dowager waved away her statement with a carefree movement of her hand. 'Very well. Keep your family secrets. They married in the end and I have seen them at various balls in London. It is apparent that it's a love match so perhaps her time here in Bath *was* for the best.'

Clara was not about to divulge her niece's secret. The secrets the Sommersby women shared with each other stayed within the family. She had never betrayed Juliet in the past and she wouldn't do so now. 'I think Juliet

and Clara knew the Collingswood sisters had come out into the garden of the house their parents had recently begun leasing next door. She wondered if Mrs Collingswood had stood by her window and peered through her sheer muslin curtains and spied them in the garden. The girls were of marrying age and she noticed that Mrs Collingswood was fond of throwing them in Clara's path whenever she had the opportunity. In fact, she had spotted them yesterday heading towards her in the Pump Room and had walked away from the fountain before Mrs Collingswood approached her, presumably hoping for an introduction to the blond-haired gentleman she had been speaking with—a man whose name she did not know.

Even though the sisters' voices weren't loud, Humphrey's sleepy head popped up and he trotted slowly towards the garden wall between the two properties.

'You left the Pump Room rather abruptly yesterday. I do hope nothing was amiss,' the Dowager said, picking up her teacup.

'No, I just saw people that I preferred to avoid and thought it best to leave before I was obligated to speak with them.'

'Nothing troubling, I hope.'

Clara leaned closer so her voice would not carry on the breeze over the garden wall. 'No, just my new neighbours,' she replied in a low whisper.

The Dowager's expression filled with interest and she, too, leaned forward. 'Neighbours can be so trying at times. Tell me about these.'

'It is the new family who are leasing the house next door.' She motioned with her head to the low garden wall where Clara suspected the Collingswood sisters were instructed to spend part of the afternoon. 'The

'My dear, he is a handsome man. I may be old, but I am not dead. What can you tell me about him?'

'The truth of the matter is that I know nothing about him. We had not been introduced before we began speaking.' Clara took a sip of tea to give her guest time to process that statement. 'You don't look shocked.'

'I'm not. I suspected as much when no introductions were made.' She tilted her head and looked Clara in the eye. The Dowager was of an advanced age, but she never seemed to miss anything that was going on around her, no matter how insignificant. 'You did speak with him, surely you must know something about him?'

'All I know is that he has spent some time in Tunbridge Wells.'

'That's all?'

Clara nodded while considering once more who he was and what had brought him to Bath.

'Did you check the registry book? Surely he must have signed the book in the Pump Room. Everyone who comes to town knows to do that.'

'There were a number of gentlemen who signed the book yesterday. There is no way to know which one he is.'

'Then you do not know how long he will be staying in Bath or if he was merely passing through.'

'I do not.'

'What a pity.' The Dowager's keen eyes settled on her again. 'I saw the way his gaze would drift to you while we stood about talking and I noticed the way you studied him when you thought none of us was looking.'

There had been a few moments when Clara was speaking with him that she had felt he was giving her his undivided attention—the way you did when you were attracted to someone. It was a lovely feeling to

number of times before he stopped and looked over at
her with those big brown eyes. She walked over to him
and picked him up. When she returned to her chair, she
placed his small body on her lap. 'Please forgive him,'
she said to the Dowager. 'He has developed a habit of
doing that. I suppose I should be grateful he does that
only to things and not people, but I don't know how to
get him to stop.' The dog in question curled into a ball
on her lap and lowered his head.

'I'm afraid I cannot help you with his problem. I've
never owned a dog. Would it help if you walked him
some more? Perhaps if you tire him out?'

'I already take him for a long walk every morning
and then I walk him at four o'clock along the Crescent
and into the park every day. It has done no good.'

The Dowager smiled up at Clara. 'I am certain you
will work out the best course of action to take. In the
meantime,' she continued, lowering her voice, 'I need
something to keep me occupied while I am here in Bath
and playing matchmaker for your neighbour's daughter
sounds like the perfect challenge. Why don't you join
me in helping her find someone special?'

'Harriet is a lovely girl. I doubt it will be a challenge.
We just need to separate her from her sister.'

'And hopefully your mystery gentleman from yesterday will still be in town and we can find out if he is
a suitable prospect for her.'

The idea that he could still be in Bath shouldn't have
mattered. He was a stranger she had spoken to for less
than thirty minutes—and yet the notion made her smile.

'The room was full of people paying five pence per glass to drink it.'

'And they go there every day?'

'Some do and drink multiple glasses. And some bathe in the hot thermal water as well.' Lane dug his hands into the pockets of his green-linen coat. 'How is it that you were the one to tell me to go to Bath and yet you know nothing about the hot springs or the Grand Pump Room?'

Hart arched his brow. 'In the seven years that you have known me, do I truly look like a person who would bathe with strange old men in ancient pools or drink water that appears to have been boiled with currency?'

'Well, no, not really.' Lane shifted in his stance.

'Then what makes you believe I know anything about the water here?'

Lane had been introduced to Hart by Lord Boundbrooke, who was on the board of the Foundling Hospital and had helped secure Lane's apprenticeship at a bank when he left the Hospital. In the years following, he had kept his eye on Lane and had told him that he thought both Lane and Hart would benefit from a friendship with each other. He was right. In Hart, he had found a rare aristocrat who didn't care that Lane did not come from a family of consequence or that he didn't even know what family he came from at all. But even though he was very fond of the man, there were times Hart could try his patience.

'You must know of the reputation of the town, Hart, and you've seen the numerous visitors that come here by the thousands because of water such as that.'

Hart brushed a lock of his black hair out of his eyes. 'Do I really have to drink this?'

'Not if you don't want to.'

Hart's blue eyes widened as his gaze travelled across the numbers. 'Surely that can't be right?'

'It is. I tell you, we need to expand. It is the logical thing to do. We need to buy The Fountain Head Hotel and then construct a bathhouse on the property. It is as if divine providence has given us a gift with that water for a reason.' He leaned in and rested his forearms on the table. 'Hart, we could make enough money to start that racecourse you and I have dreamed about. The one that will rival Ascot.'

He knew that the mention of horses would be enough of an enticement to grab his friend's interest in the project. They had been business partners for seven years. The investments he had orchestrated for them allowed his friend to live on a very nice income and not have to rely solely on his winnings at the gaming tables to support himself and now his wife as well. He knew Hart trusted his business sense, but he could still be unpredictable at times.

Lane rubbed his hand across his chin and waited.

'While we might be able to afford to purchase the hotel,' Hart said, 'we certainly can't afford the hotel *and* the construction of the bathhouse. Not after buying this place only weeks ago.'

'Do you have any ideas?'

Hart took a sip of his brandy and then stared down into his glass as if he would find his answer there. 'Sarah and I are staying with Lyonsdale and his family for a few days. I will mention it to him tonight and, should he be interested, I will arrange a meeting with the three of us. You can lay this plan of yours before him then.'

Lane rubbed his hand on his thigh as if he were rubbing out a spot on the soft buckskin of his breeches.

don't look at any more properties. We can't afford for you to get another one of your brilliant ideas.'

'I won't. This idea has my full attention. I think I'll go for a walk. After spending a good part of my afternoon in this dusty space, I could use the fresh air.'

'Lyonsdale is up near the Royal Crescent. You might want to explore that area. I don't believe there are any businesses to distract you.'

'I'll consider it.'

'You might even consider finding a woman or two. That should keep you out of trouble until you hear from me.'

'I have better things to do.' But even as he said it, an image of the woman from the Pump Room popped into his head. He consciously pushed thoughts of her aside. 'I'm determined to find a way to improve the productivity here at the coffee house. There is no sense in missing an opportunity to increase our income with this property until we change it to a spa.'

'*If* we change it over to a spa.'

'*When* we change it. I have faith that you will find a way to get us the money that we need.'

'We shall see.' Hart downed the rest of his brandy. 'Even if we get the money, what makes you believe the owner of The Fountain Head Hotel will be interested in selling it to us? I've heard it's the finest hotel in Bath and a haven for single gentlemen. With all the unmarried men visiting this town, it must turn a pretty profit.'

'They'll sell it. I'm good at brokering deals such as this and I want that property.'

tion. The tone she used to address her companion had him slowing down. What behaviour had this gentleman committed that warranted such exasperation?

'Don't look at me like that,' she continued. 'You know that I am right.'

The privet hedgerow between them was about ten inches higher than his six-foot frame and too lush to peer through the leaves to the other side.

'Honestly, I would have stayed at home if I knew this was your intention.'

The gentleman in question remained silent. Or, if he spoke, it was too low for Lane to hear. He stepped closer to the hedgerow and listened intently for any response. He heard a bit of rustling, like the sound of the fabric of a lady's skirt being moved. Although he devoted his attention to business, Lane wasn't a monk. He had lifted a skirt or two…or three or four, in his time. That was a sound that a man didn't forget.

'Oh, now you have me in a tangle. I do wish you would stop.' The woman's tone had shifted from that of exasperation to pleading.

It was in really bad form to listen to what was happening a few feet away from him. He should walk away. He should not be picturing the escapade those two were having in the woods—in the very public woods.

His thoughts flashed to an image of the woman from the Pump Room and how he had been picturing the two of them together yesterday—in the very public bath. At least his fantasy involved an empty building, after it had been closed for the day.

'Humphrey, no! Don't you do it. Humphrey!'

There was an urgency in her voice that gave him pause. Perhaps the silent Humphrey was manhandling her. Suppose she did not want him to lift her skirts

widened with apparent surprise when she saw him. 'What are *you* doing here?'

'You said you needed assistance.' He scanned the surroundings for the persistent Humphrey, but the man must have had the sense to leave before Lane made it around the hedge or he was hiding somewhere while he set his wardrobe to rights.

Apparently, this woman would probably think nothing of having a scandalous encounter in the public baths. And that thought only served to have him picturing her smooth skin glistening with the steaming bath water once more.

It was bad enough Clara was in the predicament she was in. Did she really need to be stuck like this in front of the handsome gentleman from the Pump Room?

Humphrey's leash had got tangled in the privet hedge and, if that wasn't annoying enough, when she went to try to untangle it the back of her dress had got caught on a branch as well. She had tried to release it, but that particular section of lace was at a point of her back that she couldn't reach.

When the gentleman called out to her through the hedgerow, she hesitated at first to answer. A scoundrel could take advantage of her very precarious predicament. She could be robbed, or worse. Hoping that if he tried anything, her small puppy would bite his ankles and scare him off, she accepted his invitation of assistance. Only now her puppy had disappeared into the hedge and the possible scoundrel turned out to be the man the Dowager wanted her to introduce to her neighbour.

'How can I help?' he asked, tilting his head a bit as he looked at her with a furrowed brow.

'You already have.'

She lifted her chin and now their mouths were a few inches apart. The warm air of his breath brushed across her lips. The last time she had kissed a man was ten years ago. And even then, she couldn't ever recall her pulse beating like this at the thought of kissing her husband.

Just a few more inches and their lips would be touching. Just a few more inches and she would wrap her arms around his neck and let herself sink into his embrace.

His arms tightened around hers and she felt the tugging of the back of her dress. 'I think I have it,' he said, his breath caressing her lips.

So close, their lips were so close.

A loud yapping broke the moment and the gentleman she was thinking of kissing reeled back and it was then that she realised she was free. Free of the shrub and the spell that had been cast over her. Free of desires that left her forgetting where she was or the fact that she didn't know who she was with.

She was a respectable widow and respectable women did not go around kissing gentlemen behind some shrubbery in a public park.

Humphrey's small black and brown body was hidden within the bottom branches of the thick hedge beside her, but his little black head and brown ears were visible. He continued to bark at the gentleman who had come to her aid.

'Where did you come from?' He looked between the small dog and Ciara. 'You might want to step away. It doesn't appear very friendly.'

'It's fine. He's fine. He belongs to me.' She looked down at Humphrey. 'Now hush. The nice gentleman

from the dog's collar into the hedge and moved some of the branches around to study the tangled mess. 'How did he do this?' he asked, his attention still focused on untangling the cord.

'I'm not sure. He was chasing a butterfly and the next thing I knew I was pulled practically into the bush.'

'Your leash is too long. You need a shorter one.' He motioned for her to hand him her end and then he worked it through the branches.

Not wanting to inadvertently get caught in the bushes again, Clara adjusted her blue shawl around her shoulders. 'Do you think you will be able to free him or should we just untie the leash from his collar?'

'I think I've got it. Just a few more twists… There, he is free.'

He handed her the end of the leash just as Humphrey let out a few barks before charging the gentleman's leg and resting his paws on his knee. He was rewarded with some scratching behind his ears and Humphrey whipped his head around and licked the man's hand.

'No more chasing butterflies for you, young man.'

Humphrey gave an excited bark as if to say he agreed the adventure had not been worth it.

Clara took a step closer to them and prayed Humphrey would not embarrass her with more of his inappropriate displays. 'Thank you very much for your assistance. I'm not sure what we would have done if you had not come along.'

'Well, I'm just glad I did.' He moved his hands to scratch Humphrey's neck and the little dog wagged his tail.

'Humphrey loves having his neck scratched. If you keep doing that, he won't allow you to get up.'

He looked up at her. 'Humphrey? This is Humphrey?'

is not typically frequented by visitors. They normally enjoy promenading up by the Crescent.'

'Crawling might be a better word. They were moving much too slowly for my liking.' He took a step closer.

'Moving at a sedate pace can be enjoyable when you find your companions entertaining.'

His eyes held hers for a few heartbeats before he looked around for Humphrey. 'But when you are alone and have some place to be, walking behind people being entertained is irritating.'

The candid statement was made with such a gruff delivery it almost made her laugh. 'I imagine it would be. So where did you need to be?'

'Today?'

She nodded and waited for him to respond.

'Nowhere…exactly. But that doesn't mean it was any less bothersome.'

A small laugh crept out before she could hold it back. 'So, you came here to avoid the people out there enjoying themselves.'

His brows drew together and he crossed his arms. Standing tall with his legs apart, he appeared to be preparing for battle. 'You seem to enjoy having fun at my expense.'

'I am not having fun at your expense. But you must admit you take the most benign things quite seriously.'

'I do not.'

'You do. I have lived most of my life in this town and not once have I witnessed anyone inspect the water as carefully as you did yesterday. And today you couldn't even enjoy a walk along the Crescent.'

'That does not mean I have a serious disposition.'

She crossed her arms in return. 'How would your friends describe you?'

'That's a much too leisurely way to spend my days.'

'Well, you could always attend the dress and fancy balls in the evenings in the Upper Assembly Rooms. I prefer the dress balls, myself. And there are cards rooms at those if you do not dance.'

'What makes you think I do not know how to dance?'

'Forgive me. I meant if you were not inclined to dance.'

'I find balls rather tedious. Too much talking about the weather and the state of the roads.'

'Of course. Who would want to speak to all those people enjoying each other's company?'

His lips pressed together which made her laugh again.

'Then perhaps you would prefer a concert or the theatre. Bath has a vast array of ways to entertain yourself while you are here. Your wife might enjoy those activities.' She waited to see if he would confirm that he was married. It hadn't occurred to her that he might be until now.

'Was that your way of finding out if I am married?'

She was not one to hide her inquisitive nature so she smiled up at him. 'Are you?'

Instead of appearing affronted by her question, the hint of a small smile played on his lips. 'No. I am not.'

'Neither am I.' Clara held back a groan. Why, oh, why had she offered that bit of information? It wasn't as if he had bothered to ask her.

'I know. I assumed from the Pump Room that you are widowed. I'm sorry for your loss.'

'Thank you, but my husband passed a long time ago.'

The small creases at the corners of his eyes deepened as they looked at one another.

Humphrey's head nudged her ankle, drawing her attention down to her dog. When she saw him eyeing the gentleman's boot with that expression she had come to

slowly walk away from him with her small dog trot-
ting along beside her until she reached the end of the
hedge where the dirt path they were on merged with
the gravel pathway that would take her out of the park.

There was something about being around her that
had him wanting to talk with her some more and not
rush back to the coffee house as he had originally intended. But now, running back to the coffee house was
the furthest thing from his mind as he wondered if she
walked her dog here often. When he reached the edge
of the wooded park, he looked left and right, trying to
catch sight of her, but to no avail. She was nowhere to
be found. Digging his hands into his pockets, he re-
sumed his walk. This time he didn't mind the slow pace,
since, instead of focusing on reaching his destination,
his mind was filled with thoughts of Mrs Sommersby.
And the fact that for those few moments she was stuck
to the bush, more than anything, he had wanted to kiss
her.

'Because I have been coming to Bath for years and I see the changes that are taking place here. How many times have you been to Bath, Lane?'

'I just started visiting recently.'

'I see. Well, let me tell you what I've observed. This town was once overflowing with members of the *ton*. Parading along the Crescent resembled making your way through the crowds at Almack's on a Wednesday night. But do you know what I see now?'

Lane shook his head, wishing that he could tell Lyonsdale that he didn't want to know. Those numbers on that page spoke louder to him.

'Now I see a town fading somewhat in its glory as the most fashionable place to be outside of London. There are not nearly as many members of the *ton* here as there once were. Brighton is where the Regent is. Brighton is where the growth is. Do not mistake what I am saying. Bath is still a desirable destination, but for how much longer? It may be profitable now, but can you truly tell me it will continue to be profitable ten years from now...or twenty?'

While Lyonsdale, unlike many members of English Society, always treated Lane with respect, Lane had never felt the divide in class as acutely with the man as he did at this very moment.

'There are no guarantees in business,' Lane replied, looking Lyonsdale directly in the eye. 'I cannot say with one hundred per cent certainty that this venture will be profitable ten years from now or twenty. But what I can guarantee is that right now...now, those numbers are sound. And while people of your class and position may not be flocking here the way they once were, people of my class are. The merchant class and those who are discovering ways to make money through in-

head as he pinched the bridge of his nose. By keeping his head lowered and not looking at Lane, it was apparent he was contemplating where he would hit Lane first, once Lyonsdale left.

Silence descended over them, cloaking the room with an air of foreboding.

Finally, the Duke let out a loud breath. 'You can pick your head up, Hart. I'm not about to storm out. This is just becoming entertaining.'

While Hart's head jerked up, Lane had the urge to reach across the table and plant a facer on Lyonsdale. He was not entertaining. None of this was entertaining. Why were people all of a sudden considering him entertaining? First Mrs Sommersby and now Lyonsdale.

'And stand down, Lane. I did not mean to imply that the world outside my circle isn't important. But certainly you know that the *ton* sets the fashion for the rest of England. If those of English Society move out of Bath completely, it will only be a matter of time before others follow suit. That was what I meant. My comments were not intended to disparage anyone with a position in Society under me.'

The tension in Lane's shoulders began to ease a bit even though Lyonsdale was right. Lane was not an unreasonable man. To succeed in business, you had to have an open mind and view a situation from another point of view. 'It is a valid point—however, I have been to the spas. They are filled with the infirm and aged. And they keep coming. This is not just a town that attracts people for the fashionable entertainments. This is a town that people believe will cure their ills. I cannot say if they are right or wrong. I have not witnessed it myself, but what I have seen is the look in the eyes of those who I have spoken to that shine with hope. A hope

how much money Lyonsdale will give us to build the spa.' He raised a challenging brow at him and smirked.

Before his interest waned or Hart provoked him too far, Lane needed to secure Lyonsdale to this project. 'Do you now see the potential we have here?' he asked, taking the Duke's attention away from Hart.

Lyonsdale drew the sheet of paper with the budget closer to him and his gaze slowly moved from side to side as he scanned the page. When he sat back, it was Lane whom he focused on. 'I will fund some of this, but I am not willing to give you all the money you need. And it will be on loan to you for five years.'

When he told them the amount of what he was willing to give and the interest he would charge them, Lane's heart sank. It was not an unusual arrangement that Lyonsdale had offered. Most of the time Lyonsdale preferred to be conservative in his investments. It was just that this time—with this opportunity—Lane had hoped Lyonsdale would see the full potential and take the risk.

'Come now,' Hart said, breaking his self-imposed silence. 'If you give us the full amount we think we will need, then you can become a full partner and reap all the rewards when this spa becomes the sensation of all of Bath and word of it hits London and this town becomes fashionable again.'

'I thought you were going to sit there and offer your silent support?' Lyonsdale said, shifting his weight on his chair away from Hart.

'You knew that was never going to happen, so there is no need to pretend you expected it to. It is early in the morning. You haven't had your breakfast yet. Why don't you go home, have something to eat and think about it some more?'

Chapter Six

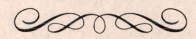

The Lower Assembly Rooms were located close to the banks of the River Avon, not far from the King's and Queen's Baths and Bath Abbey. The large room Lane found himself in with the tall windows held balls on Tuesday and Thursday evenings, according to Hart. It wasn't until they stepped inside that he recalled Mrs Sommersby mentioning it to him when they spoke in the park.

While they were being escorted past the small round tables of two-to-four people to get to their seats, he found himself scanning the occupants to see if she were here and found it oddly disconcerting when his spirits dropped even more than they already had when he didn't see her.

'Have something to eat. It might help to improve that mood you're in,' Hart said after they settled in with their steaming mugs of coffee and buttery-smelling breads.

'I'm fine.'

'You don't appear to be fine. You look as if you will rip apart our waiter should he offer you more coffee. Which is rather inconvenient since I believe I will be having more than one cup.'

'Correction. I was a complicated wreck. Now, I'm just complicated.'

'How does Sarah live with you?'

'She finds my complications endearing.'

'At least someone does.' To avoid having to look at Hart's cocky grin, he turned his attention away from his friend.

And spotted Mrs Sommersby, sitting not far from them.

She was wearing a pink and green dress as she sat with a red-haired young woman. Both women appeared to be enjoying each other's company as they placed their orders with their waiter.

'…are much less conservative in their investing than Lyonsdale,' he heard Hart say, breaking into his study of Mrs Sommersby. 'I believe there is a good chance that I can get them to commit to this.'

'Who?'

'Weren't you listening to me?' Hart scanned the area of the room where Mrs Sommersby sat as if he were trying to determine what had captured Lane's attention. With so many people sitting near them, it would be impossible for him to work it out. Hart must have come to that conclusion as well, since he looked back at Lane. 'I'll be heading back to London in two days to handle some additional affairs that need my attention and will speak with a number of potential investors then. Hopefully, soon, we will have the funds we need to create this spa of yours.'

At the mention of the spa, Lane found it hard to swallow the bread in his mouth. 'Hopefully they will be more willing to invest in it than Lyonsdale was.'

Not wishing to dwell any further on his aggravating day, Lane's attention was drawn back to Mrs Sommersby, who was now speaking in an animated fashion to her

so he would just stop talking, Lane took a sip of coffee and waited.

His friend chose that very moment to take a bite of bread, prolonging the time it took him to answer. 'I don't remember my exact words.'

'Well...what is it that you think you might have said to her?'

'Well... I *think* I might have asked if she'd care to take a turn with me in the darkened gardens during a ball we attended together. It was probably a cold night and I may have offered to keep her warm as we looked at the stars.'

'Have you had much success with that suggestion?'

'You'd be surprised.' Hart took another bite of bread.

An inexplicable lump formed in Lane's throat. 'So you are intimately acquainted with the woman?'

'Mrs Sommersby?' Hart shook his head. 'No, I thought you were just referring to the suggestion in itself. I'd had a bit of success with it in the past.'

'But not with her?'

Once again, Hart shook his head, but this time the movement was slower. 'No, no. If I recall correctly, she was flattered, but I am certain she definitely declined.' Picking up his cup, he looked over to where Mrs Sommersby was sitting. 'Before Sarah, I had a marked preference for older women.'

'She's not that old,' Lane replied, sounding almost indignant, which was strange since he had no reason to feel insulted on her behalf.

'Well, she is certainly older than the girls the mothers try to throw into your path when you are an earl attending a ball, I can tell you that. I found older women more at ease with themselves and they know their desires much better than a girl out of the schoolroom usually

The waiter came to their table to clear away their plates, saving Lane from having to answer.

'Lane?'

Damn. He hated the thought that went into answering questions like this. Years ago, Lane learned no good came from analysing his feelings. It was best to move through life without thinking too much about what anything made him feel. He had become quite skilled at it.

'I do well for myself.'

The vague comment made Hart laugh. 'With the money you've made I'm sure you do and I've been told you are not hard on the eyes.'

Lane sat up a bit taller. 'By whom?'

'Miss Violet Westfield, one of Sarah's friends. She saw us together some time ago. I can introduce you when you are back in London, if you like?'

Was his wife's friend as attractive as Mrs Sommersby? Not that Mrs Sommersby was an outstanding beauty, but she was pretty and there was just something about her. He turned back to take a look to try to determine what it was.

'If we can get the funding we need, it might be some time before I'm back in London,' he replied, keeping his eyes on Mrs Sommersby.

'And your decision is based solely on your need to remain here on business?'

When Lane looked back at Hart, he wanted to hit that all-too-perceptible smirk off his face.

'Yes.'

'Hmm. Well, I'm sure you have things that you need to address back at the coffee house and I promised Sarah that I would be home by noon to go with her for a drive around the countryside, so why don't I ask for the bill and we can leave?'

him and as his friend walked towards Mrs Sommersby's table he almost wished he had done it. In true Hart
fashion, he looked back at Lane with a smile before he al-
tered his course slightly, missing the table where she sat.

Every nerve in his body was strung tight. Relying on
others was not something he was comfortable with, but
unfortunately it was part of doing business. And now
he would have to wait a week before he knew if they
could move forward with their plans.

As his vision began to clear, Mrs Sommersby came
into focus. How long he had been staring sightlessly at
her, he had no idea. She was listening intently to what
her companion was saying. What did women talk about
when they weren't in the company of men? The question
had never occurred to him until now. Once more, Lane
tried to read lips and once more he failed miserably.

She had this way of gracefully moving her fingers
as she continually spun her cup in her saucer. It was
distinctly possible that she wasn't even aware she was
doing it, but oddly enough watching her movement was
easing his agitation. Suddenly she looked his way and,
as their eyes met, a slow smile spread across her face.
Something inside him shifted and it felt as if the sun had
come out for the first time during this very gloomy day.

the urge to see if Mr Lane was still watching her. With a concerted effort, she focused all of her attention on the woman sitting across the small round table from her.

The more time Clara spent with the young woman, the more she discovered she liked her. Taking her to the spa this morning to drink the waters with her and then bringing her here to the Lower Assembly Room for breakfast had proved to be a wise decision. It had become apparent that spending time with her while Clara searched for potential husbands for the woman would be rather enjoyable.

Although, currently, it was proving to be impossible to keep her attention on her for very long. The urge to glance over at Mr Lane was too great and her gaze slid over to him once more.

His eyes were still on her.

She needed to appear composed and unaffected by his attention. She was a middle-aged woman. His attention shouldn't make her want to smile, yet it was taking great effort on her part to keep her expression neutral as she quickly looked back at Harriet. 'And your sister? Does Ann have a desire to see the play?'

'No. Ann prefers operas. She tends to favour whatever is considered the height of fashion at the moment and has heard that many women of the *ton* favour it. Have you seen any of Mr Sheridan's plays?'

'I have seen all of his work and every production.' This might be just the opportunity Clara was looking for to remove Harriet from her family long enough to introduce her to potential suitors. 'Do you think your mother will be willing to spare you for one evening? If she would, I'd be happy to take you to see it at the Theatre Royal. I have a box there.'

The invitation appeared to embarrass Harriet, who

wanted to give you a place to take that step.' She removed her hand with a pat and took a sip of her tea.

Harriet was an attractive girl with warm brown eyes and hair the colour of the setting sun. Clara knew men well enough to know that they would find her rather full lips a seductive feature, even though the young woman herself was probably unaware of the allure. Could Mr Lane have been staring at her in hopes of garnering an introduction? She already knew he wasn't married. Peering over her teacup, she moved her gaze in his direction and became disappointed when she found that he was no longer there.

However, her disappointment was short-lived when he suddenly approached her side from behind.

'Good morning, Mrs Sommersby,' he said over the sounds of the conversations going on around them.

'Mr Lane, I see you have taken my advice and come here to have breakfast.' She gave him a bright smile to show she appreciated that he had followed her recommendation.

He took a quick glance around. 'I actually accompanied a friend here. He had suggested this establishment. I stayed after he left to finish my coffee.'

There was nothing quite like humiliating yourself in front of a new friend. The man had probably forgotten all about her recommendation of this place the moment she'd left him in the park.

'Forgive me for imposing on your time,' he said with a slight hesitation, 'but you dropped this.'

When he held out her white napkin, Clara was reminded yet again that she had been a fool for thinking even for a minute that he had fancied her. As she took the napkin from him, she was careful not to brush her fingers against his so he would not assume that she

Wanting to save them all from the awkwardness of the situation, she turned away from him and signalled her waiter with the tilt of her head. 'Do enjoy the rest of your day, Mr Lane, and the remainder of your time in Bath.'

'Mrs Sommersby. Miss Collingswood.'

She felt, rather than saw, when he walked away from their table. How was she to bolster the confidence of Harriet with men like Mr Lane around? His demeanour just now was best described as gruff. For a man who had been staring at her minutes earlier to behave in such a manner when they had an opportunity to converse was puzzling.

It wasn't long before she had the chance to confront him on his behaviour when she stepped outside the Assembly Room and spotted him not far from the entrance with his hands in the pockets of his long green coat, presumably waiting for his carriage or a sedan chair.

Early on in her marriage to Robert, Clara's husband had tried to shield her when the state of their finances became grim. The dire truth during those times would often surface unexpectedly when she was in one of the shops in town. The mortification she would feel at those moments led her to understand the value of open and honest communication. And now the truth she wished she could uncover was why Mr Lane had been watching her so intently during breakfast, only to practically run from her once they spoke.

She looked over at him and adjusted the brim of her bonnet to shield her eyes from the sun that was shining high in the bright blue sky. The movement must have caught his attention, since their eyes met immediately after she lowered her gloved hands. He gave her an al-

Chapter Eight

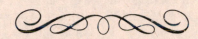

Lane knew he had behaved horribly with Mrs Sommersby, but the minute Miss Collingswood asked where he was from that defensive instinct inside him kicked in and he wanted to do whatever he could to avoid talking about himself. Miss Collingswood was much too young to have remembered him from the Foundling Hospital. It wasn't possible she was recalling the time he spent growing up there. However, whenever someone said he looked familiar, a prickling sensation would run along his skin and his instinct was to run.

He had faced many disgusted looks and received the cut from people in respectable levels of Society once they were made aware of his origins. Most of the children abandoned and left in the care of the Foundling Hospital were there because they were by-blows whose fathers would not or could not marry their mothers. This was common knowledge and it changed how many people treated you when they found out you were raised there. From the time that he was a young child, Lane had formed a hard shell around his emotions. But today, that shell had a crack in it and deep down he knew for some reason he didn't want Mrs Sommersby to treat him that way.

apology and I am sorry I placed you in an awkward position. I assumed you were in a better disposition and even thought you might have actually smiled at me while you were drinking your coffee.'

Had he smiled at her? It had brightened his day when he had spotted her...but shortly afterwards he remembered his discussion with Lyonsdale and knew his time was better spent attending to business. 'I had received some disappointing news this morning. My friend thought having breakfast here would improve my disposition. I believe you would say that it has not.'

'I hope it was not bad news from home. Your family is well?' Concern was etched on her face and shone in her amber-coloured eyes.

'It was nothing like that. It was a business matter.' That was one more reminder today that, unlike most people, he had no family.

'I see. Well I am sorry none the less.'

A shiny black-lacquered carriage pulled up and she held up her finger to the driver, indicating she would be a moment longer. She bit her lip and appeared to be deciding if she should say something else to him. He arched his brow in encouragement and waited.

'Would you consider allowing me to try to improve your current grumpy state?'

'I don't believe we agreed I was exactly grumpy, but tell me what you had in mind.'

'Tomorrow night I will be attending a performance of *The Rivals* at the Theatre Royal, not far from here. It's a wonderful play by Mr Sheridan and one that I believe might lift your spirits. If you are still in town, would you like to join me at the theatre to see it?'

Lane couldn't remember the last time he was in a theatre. There was no sense in attending plays when he

Chapter Nine

The next afternoon Clara sat in the back garden of The Fountain Head Hotel across the table from her cousin Phillip Edwards, trying a new selection of bread that the hotel's cook had been interested in serving during breakfast. While Clara owned the hotel, it was Phillip who managed it for her and gave a face to the public of being the probable owner.

She moved in elevated social circles. One of her three nieces was a duchess. She herself had been married to the youngest son of an earl who had seen it as beneath him to own a lodging establishment and that was why when he was alive he never agreed with her that it was a wise investment when they had the funds. If word got out that she owned a hotel, she would be shunned by members of the *ton*, the very Society her family moved in, and she had no desire to bring any shame to those nieces whom she loved as if they were her own daughters. And when she was serving as chaperone for her unmarried niece, she would never have taken the chance of hurting Juliet's ability to make a strong match.

Phillip had agreed to run the hotel for her when she had purchased it not long after she became a widow and

tea, which had cooled in her cup since they began this discussion. To those around them who knew them, it appeared to be a monthly family meal shared by the two cousins.

'But I disagree. We shall try it for a month. If in that time we find that it is not to our benefit, we change the menu back.'

His round face looked pinched as he stared across the table at her as if he were suffering from an aching head. 'Very well. Write up a menu and I'll discuss it with the cook.'

She could tell by his expression that he did not believe it would succeed. Even though the hotel was putting a good amount of money in her pocket every month, it was important to her to look for ways to make certain it remained a desirable place to stay. This hotel was everything to her.

The remainder of the day seemed to crawl by as she looked forward to heading to the theatre that night. Finally, at seven p.m., she entered her carriage with Harriet to see the opening-night performance of Sheridan's play.

'I have invited a few friends to join us tonight. It will give you an opportunity to meet some other people here in Bath.'

A flicker of nervous uncertainty crossed Harriet's face in the dim light of the rocking carriage. 'I hope you didn't go to any trouble for me. I know that my mother expressed an interest in meeting as many people as we can while we are here, but I am not of the same nature.'

'It was no trouble. I have asked Mr Lane to join us.'

the mood to chat with poor Harriet. 'It might be in our best interest to evaluate Mr Lane's disposition before trying to start a conversation with him.'

'And how are we to do that if we cannot speak with him?'

'There are other signs besides his speech that will be an indication.'

'Such as?'

'Harriet, can you tell when your father is out of sorts when he walks into a room?'

'Usually.'

'Well, most men are the same. Pay close attention to the line of his brow. One can typically tell a lot about a person by their eyes.'

Her friend looked down and picked at her pale blue silk glove. 'I think I will wait to say anything to him until I see how you proceed.'

'Very well, if it makes you feel more at ease, then follow my lead. I assure you, you will have no problems with the Dowager Duchess of Lyonsdale. She will be joining us as well and she is delightful.'

'A dowager duchess?' There was a distinct crack in Harriet's voice and her hands flew to her stomach. 'There really was no need to invite these people for my sake.'

'I assure you, she is lovely.'

'Maybe to people who have vouchers at Almack's, but my father is a barrister.'

'That's a very noble profession, Harriet.'

'Yes, but she is a duchess.'

'I would not invite people who I thought would make you feel uncomfortable.'

'Mr Lane already made me feel uncomfortable.'

nity to meet. May I introduce you both to Mr Greeley. Mr Greeley, this is Mrs Sommersby and Miss Collingswood. Mr Greeley is the grandson of Sir Percy Fullerton, an old friend.'

Harriet seemed frozen in place as she watched Mr Greeley extend his greeting.

'Greeley, why don't you point out the new lights on the stage to Miss Collingswood that you were showing me earlier?' the Dowager said, arching her brow at him. 'He has assured me, Miss Collingswood, they are a bit extraordinary. I cannot explain them myself, but he knows a lot about them. Apparently, this theatre was built almost twenty years ago and he knows one of the architects personally. Isn't that right?' She gave him an encouraging smile.

The poor man had been staring at Harriet and the Dowager's words seemed to bring him out of his stupor. 'Oh, yes. Mr Palmer was a family friend. He would tell me about building this theatre when I was a young boy. Hearing those stories helped develop my interest in architecture.'

Harriet was smiling a bit shyly at him. 'I like architecture as well, Mr Greeley. I am a great admirer of Mr Adam's work. I have a fondness for the classical designs.'

Apparently, her statement was met with approval from Mr Greeley, who was practically beaming. 'I've studied his work extensively. You have excellent taste, Miss Collingswood.'

'Greeley is an architect,' the Dowager interjected. 'And a fine one at that. He will be working on a number of follies on the grounds of Lyonsdale Hall later this year. Katrina, my grandson's wife, was very happy with his designs.'

'I've invited a gentleman here tonight as well.' Now this could prove to be a bit awkward since Clara wasn't certain what she expected to happen between Harriet and Mr Lane.

'You have? Why did you not tell me?'

'I didn't think I needed to. I thought you were going to leave things up to me. He is the gentleman from out of town who we spoke about from the Pump Room. His name is Mr Lane.'

The Dowager brought her gloved hands together, eliciting a muffled clap. 'Capital! A girl should always have the option of choosing from more than one suitor.'

'I wouldn't exactly call him—'

'They do seem to be getting on rather well.' The Dowager motioned to Harriet and Mr Greeley who had their heads bent together in an animated discussion. 'Don't you think?'

'Well, yes, but I thought you were going to let me find her a suitor.'

'I told you I was bored here in Bath and needed something to occupy my time.' She dipped her chin into an almost coquettish look.

'I know what you're about. You want to see who is the better matchmaker.'

'That thought never crossed my mind.' Yet her expression told a different tale.

'What made you think Mr Greeley would be suitable for Miss Collingswood?'

'Have you not looked at him? My dear, he is a quite pleasing young man. Even at my advanced age I can see that.'

'Is that all he has to recommend him?'

'No. He has a charming manner, is affable, has a budding career as an architect and his father is a well-respected

during breakfast. I was inspired.' That inspiration had more to do with giving Harriet opportunities to feel comfortable conversing with a gentleman than it did with arranging a courtship.

'I see. Well, we will have to wait and see which one she prefers.'

From the time she was a young girl, Clara had had a competitive streak. It was not her finest quality to be sure, but it was a part of her that would surface every now and then. And right now that part of her nature was screaming that she was a better matchmaker.

Looking over at Harriet, she found her listening intently to what Mr Greeley was saying while their heads were lowered close to one another. She looked very comfortable and happy with him. Less than an hour ago she looked as if she had wanted to jump out of the carriage when Clara mentioned that she would be seeing Mr Lane again.

If she were to seriously propose Mr Lane as a potential suitor, she needed to know far more about him than she already did. She knew nothing of his background. She didn't know where he lived, aside from London, or anything about his family. He was a businessman, but what kind of business was he involved in? And she still needed to find a way to repair the damage he had done with his brusque manner yesterday.

Clara did not like losing and she did have a skill for matching up suitable partners. Mr Lane was handsome, at times charming, and she knew he hid a wonderful dry sense of humour. She got the impression he was an intelligent man. And while he might not be a gentleman who favoured the very latest fashion, the cut of his clothes showed off his athletic form and she could tell they were well made. And he was just the right height

Chapter Ten

Lane was not fond of crowds. But he had given his word to Mrs Sommersby that he would be here and he never went back on his word. However, the next time someone invited him out to a social engagement, he would find a reason to decline. It was moments like this that he was reminded why he preferred to stay in at night. He had a much better time obsessing over his business ventures.

Tonight, for example, he could have been relaxing in his office at the coffee house and drinking some fine Madeira while he read the profit and loss statement for the racing stables he owned with Hart in York. Just because he was consumed with the idea of building a spa here in Bath didn't mean he could afford to neglect his other ventures. They needed his attention as well. He wouldn't risk handing over complete control of these businesses to someone else and take the chance that they might run them into the ground. He grew up having nothing to call his own. He would never allow that to happen again. That's why he was very selective about where he chose to invest his time and money.

But now, instead of scrutinising the expenses of the stables, he was making his way up the stairs to Mrs

There was something about Mrs Sommersby that took him away from obsessing about his work and relieved some of the pressure he felt on a daily basis. While he knew he should be home reading that report, he found his chest felt lighter when she was around—and he liked that. The idea that she might cut all ties with him should she find out that he was born on the other side of the blanket, probably to a servant girl, made his stomach drop. His pride had already been dented this week by his disagreement with Lyonsdale. He wasn't about to take another blow. The Dowager didn't need to know that he knew her grandson.

While Lane lowered his head in a respectable bow, he spotted a man and a woman sitting in two of the chairs in the front row of the box. How was it possible that he had assumed he would be spending the evening alone with Mrs Sommersby and she had an entirely different evening planned? He tried to recall her exact words when she invited him to join her tonight, but couldn't.

'It is a pleasure to formally make your acquaintance, Mr Lane,' the Dowager said with a warm smile, reminding him how surprisingly affable she had been when they stood around the fountain. 'I hope you found the water you drank to be beneficial in some way.'

'My morning at the spa was very beneficial. Thank you.'

'Capital! You should try bathing in it. It can be very restorative. Isn't that right?' she said, turning to Mrs Sommersby.

'I've found it to be.'

Once more the image of Mrs Sommersby in the hot spring bath popped into his mind and once more he wished he was spending the evening alone with her.

The Dowager took a step back. 'If you two will ex-

Thankfully, Miss Collingswood was tucked into the corner beside Mr Greeley in the last seat in the row, so he didn't have to worry that anyone was considering him as a potential suitor for her. Over the years he had come to realise that there were those people who assumed, because he was a bachelor, that he was looking for a wife. He had been abandoned once in his life by a woman. He was not eager to put himself in a situation where it could happen again. At seven and thirty he had become very skilled at avoiding the matchmaking mothers who valued his wealth over the circumstances of his birth.

As they went to sit down, it was Mrs Sommersby's turn to wrinkle her brow when she took note that the two vacant chairs were on the other side of the Dowager. 'We could sit behind Miss Collingswood and Mr Greeley,' she offered.

'Or we could sit in the front row and have a better view of the stage.'

'Oh, quite right. I just thought this might be more conducive to conversation.'

'Do you frequently talk during a performance?'

'Well, no. Do you?'

'I can't recall the last time I went to the theatre, but I doubt I spent much time talking.'

'Now that I can believe,' she replied over her shoulder in a teasing tone as she made her way to the chair beside the Dowager.

Just as Lane took his seat next to her, the red-velvet curtain on the stage came up. With everyone's attention fixed on the actors, Lane closed his eyes and hoped that his head wouldn't bob if he nodded off to sleep. He had been up well before sunrise today, observing the delivery process of the coffee and sugar at the coffee house and reviewing with his manager the amounts ordered. No

'Who?'

'Miss Collingswood.'

'Greeley seems to think so. Are they engaged?'

'Greeley and Miss Collingswood? No, they just met this evening. I don't even know if she likes him.'

'Ah, so it truly is a matter of art imitating life. Well, you have nothing to fear. You seem to have made a good match.'

Her eyes widened as she brought her fan up to her chest. 'You misunderstand. I am not trying to foster a match between them.'

None of the women he knew were matchmakers. At least he hadn't witnessed any attempting such a feat. And if they did, he doubted they would have confessed as much to him.

'Are you saying I'm Mrs Malapropism in this scenario?' she continued with low indignation. 'The one who in that scene was just accused of being an old weather-beaten she-dragon guarding her charge? The one who was accused of being vain with coarse features? The one who uses words incorrectly?' Her voice was low, but sharp, and there was a distinct possibility she was about to hit him with her fan.

Although they were in a crowded theatre, it felt inexplicably as if they were all alone. He leaned his head close to hers and she did not back away. 'You are far too young to be accused of being old and weather-beaten.'

'But I am still a vain she-dragon with coarse features? That makes it all so much better.' She rolled her eyes at him before snapping open her fan so sharply that he had to lean back or it might have struck his nose.

'I assure you that no one would accuse you of any of those things.'

'I believe, Mr Lane, that I prefer you when you say

have believed her, she held it up to show her for good measure. 'The production has been wonderful so far.'

The Dowager shifted her attention between the two of them before settling on Lane. 'And are you enjoying it?'

He tried to swallow away the dryness in his mouth. 'Quite, thank you.' It would have been more enjoyable if his moment with Mrs Sommersby hadn't been interrupted and even more so if they had been alone. It was hard to stop imagining her soft lips against his.

'Oh, it is simply a wonderful play,' Miss Collingswood exclaimed, practically jumping into the seats behind them with Mr Greeley. 'Don't you agree, Mrs Sommersby? Thank you for asking me to join you here tonight. I am so thrilled that I did not have to miss it.'

'I'm glad that tonight has brought you so much joy,' Mrs Sommersby replied with what almost appeared to be a pleased maternal expression.

'And you, Mr Greeley,' the Dowager addressed the man who was younger than Lane. 'Are you enjoying the play?'

'Yes, Your Grace. Mr Sheridan has done a fine job capturing the foibles of courtship.'

'Let us hope all courtships aren't like that,' she replied. 'I would like to believe that most people are not filled with artifice.'

'But don't you think most are, in some way?' Lane chimed in.

Mrs Sommersby looked as if she were studying him. 'I suppose. People tend to show only the best of themselves in the beginning, not wanting to do anything that will push the other person away.'

'But is that truly artifice,' the Dowager asked, 'or is it simply being on your best behaviour?'

'I think it might be more. Everyone has skeletons

should you disclose that to Miss Collingswood now for the sake of honesty or wait until a later date when you are confident that she has affection for you?'

Mr Greeley looked nervously at Miss Collingswood as if it had been revealed to the entire theatre that the man did pick his teeth with his fork.

The orchestra struck up a few chords, letting the people milling about in the corridors and visiting other boxes know that the performance was about to resume, saving Mr Greeley from continuing the conversation. The noise in the theatre grew louder with the sounds of people returning to their seats and as the young couple moved back to their chairs, Lane exchanged a small smile with Mrs Sommersby.

'One has to wonder if Mr Greeley does indeed pick his teeth with a fork,' she said low enough so only he could hear her behind her fan.

'With his truly honourable nature, he is probably confessing it to her as we speak.'

They both leaned out to see past the Dowager and watched the couple deep in conversation. Whatever they were discussing didn't seem to bother Miss Collingswood since she still appeared to be in very good spirits.

The Dowager waved her gloved hand at Lane and Mrs Sommersby. The diamonds in her substantial bracelet sparkled in the candlelight. 'Leave them alone, you two. We all have skeletons as Mr Lane has said.'

'Yes, but mine do not have cutlery,' he replied, sitting back in his chair and settling in, missing the amused expressions the ladies shared.

kissing him would have felt like when her arm acci-
dently brushed against his rather solid one, encased in
his black tailcoat. Their eyes held for a moment before
she looked down and brushed out the wrinkles from
her skirt and opened her fan, hoping to cool the flush
spreading throughout her body from that one spot on
her arm where his body had touched hers.

He looked very handsome in his formal black evening
attire. The jacket and trousers were cut well, showing off
his broad shoulders and well-defined form. His cravat had
a nice fall to it and his cheeks and jaw were so smooth they
must have been freshly shaven. One thing that she found
herself continually drawn to was this commanding pres-
ence he had about him that led her to believe that he was
the type of gentleman who faced his problems head on and
would not run away from them. From her marriage, she
was more accustomed to the uneasy feeling she got around
a gentleman who would run. Her late husband, God rest
his soul, had frequently hid from their creditors. That had
forced Clara to be the one to try to placate the shopkeep-
ers in town during those times when they were short on
funds to settle their bills. She was the one who made sure
they weren't thrown in debtors' prison. What would her
life have been like had she married a man like Mr Lane?

She really didn't know anything about him. Perhaps he
wasn't as financially solvent as she would have liked to
believe. Over the years she had helped to encourage the
courtships of a number of women and she had developed
a keen sense for how to analyse a person. Lowering her
eyelids, she took note of the condition of his sleeve and the
fact that it was not threadbare. The cuff of his linen shirt
that peeked out from the cuff of his coat was pure white,
telling her that he was both clean and financially solvent
enough to pay someone to have his clothes washed. He

The hush came from the Dowager, making Clara feel as though she was younger than Harriet.

There were so many questions she suddenly wanted answers to. There were so many things she did not know. And, oh, how she wished she could ask him about all of them. However, if there was one thing she knew for certain, it was that Mr Lane did not appear to be a gentleman who liked talking about himself.

They sat side by side and watched the remainder of the play together. Occasionally, they would share a smile over something that was happening on the stage. And at times she felt acutely aware of his body so close to hers, which would prompt her to fan herself and hope the flush she was feeling was not that noticeable. When the curtain went down one final time, she leaned her shoulder towards his, wondering if he regretted accepting her invitation this evening. 'Are you glad that you stayed awake tonight?'

'Surprisingly, I am.'

'And would you agree that coming here tonight was a better way to spend your evening than the way you had planned to spend it?'

He looked as if he were actually trying to determine if it were—which felt rather insulting—and made her very curious.

'What was it that you were planning on doing tonight?'

'I was going to review a business report.'

'Ah, business. The mysterious thing that keeps you so busy and has prevented you from enjoying your time here. What was the report about?'

They stood up to join the rest of their party by the door to the box.

a reprieve of spending more time with me until my carriage arrives. Then he will be forced to endure my chatter all the way home.' She was watching Mr Greeley and Harriet with marked interest, which reminded Clara about the woman's challenge to see who would find the more desirable suitor for the young woman.

'I assure you it will be my pleasure to ride back with you,' Mr Greeley replied with a tip of his head before turning to Clara. 'Mrs Sommersby, Miss Collingswood, might I have the honour of escorting you both outside?'

Harriet took his right arm, leaving Clara with his left. The staircase was wide enough to accommodate the three of them as they made their descent, but when they reached the door, Clara let go of his arm so they could fit through the door to the outside. She threaded both her hands through the braided handle of her reticule as they waited on the pavement for the three carriages to arrive.

The Dowager's carriage arrived first and, after she bade them a safe trip home, Clara stood alone outside with Harriet and Mr Lane. It appeared they were some of the last to leave the theatre since there was only one other small group of people standing about twenty feet from them. The yellow glow from the lights inside the building shone on to the narrow strip of pavement they were standing on, making it easier for them to see each other in the darkness that surrounded them.

'Will it be a far drive for you, Mr Lane?' Harriet enquired, seeming to have completely lost her trepidation about the gentleman.

'Not too far.' He stuffed his hands in the pockets of his coat. 'Will you have a far drive ahead of you?'

'My family is staying next door to Mrs Sommersby. It should not take us long before we are home.'

Mr Lane's carriage pulled alongside the pavement

tention? 'You comported yourself very well. So, you are fond of Mr Lane?'

'I am. I think he is a fine man.'

'I agree.'

'And very handsome.'

What? 'You do? Think he is handsome, that is?'

'Yes. Don't you?'

'Well, yes I suppose.'

'You suppose?' Harriet's eyebrows rose. 'He has such well-defined features, unmarked skin and such a strong square jaw. And that hair of his appears to be so thick you could start to comb your fingers through it and not finish until the next day. Oh, and have I mentioned that he has a very fine form...if one was to notice such things.'

'I truly did not look to see.' Which was a lie. Of course she'd noticed what a fine specimen of a man he was. It was hard not to when she was sitting close beside him and when she was close enough to kiss him. 'Tell me your thoughts on Mr Greeley.'

'Mr Greeley is a lovely man,' she replied with a carefree wave of her hand. 'I'm not saying he is not, I just think that a woman would be lucky to marry a man like Mr Lane.' She tilted her head and looked at Clara as if she were waiting for her reaction.

The distant cry of the night watchman carried through the carriage with an 'all is well.' It was well, wasn't it? She had considered matching Harriet with Mr Lane. She was even challenged to do so by the Dowager. And now it appeared it would be no problem at all to convince Harriet to consider him. That should have made her feel good. She should be delighted and relieved that Harriet found him handsome.

Clara looked out into the darkened night and her gaze roamed over the windows of the terraced town

to Sydney Gardens? She certainly had not left an impression on him if that was where he was going. If he'd had a desire to see her again, he would have made certain to walk near the Crescent. Not that it mattered. She was not looking for a gentleman of her own and, even if she were, she was too old for him anyway. A gentleman as young as Mr Lane would want a family. That was something she could not give him.

For Harriet's sake, she should try to locate him and find a way to bring them together again. This time Harriet should have an opportunity to spend time with him without Mr Greeley there to muddy the waters.

'I could take Humphrey for a walk in Sydney Gardens tomorrow on the chance that he might be there,' she offered. 'He did seem to enjoy himself this evening. I don't think he would mind if I invited him to something else.'

Harriet sat up taller. 'I think you should.' She really was more attracted to him than Clara had thought.

Just the idea of seeing him again had her opening up her fan. She would have to approach this delicately. If possible, she needed to find something that she could do with Harriet that did not involve her family. The last thing she wanted was for her mother to throw her sister Ann in his path which might have Harriet retreating back into her shell.

There was still more she needed to find out about him before she could recommend him to Mr and Mrs Collingswood. If she needed to spend more time with him to do that, she would find the time for Harriet's sake, though, she didn't want Mr Lane to feel like a hunted man. There was no reason he should think of her as Mrs Malapropism from the play. She was no she-

Chapter Twelve

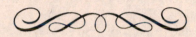

The desire to remain in bed after the sun came up was a new one for Lane. When he was a child, he would be woken up at seven each morning to have enough time to dress and make it down to the dining hall for breakfast. Even now, as an adult, he never slept past six.

But this morning as he lay in his bed in his room in The Fountain Head Hotel and watched the sky change colour outside his window, going from inky black to orange streaked with red, he rested his head in the crook of his arm and thought again about last night. And those thoughts were making him want to remain in bed for as long as he could.

The image of Mrs Sommersby was fresh in his mind. He could still picture her intelligent eyes and amused expression as she sat beside him in her deep blue satin gown that cradled her breasts and skimmed along the rest of her body. The soft scent of roses still somehow seemed to linger in his nose and, if he closed his eyes, he could imagine the puff of her soft, warm breath near his ear that he had felt each time she would lean over to whisper to him.

She had asked if his family had ever brought him to the theatre. It never occurred to him that families would

'As long as I've been. I've heard he is from Bath, though, so perhaps a long time.'

'You did not grow up here?'

'Me? No, sir. I'm from London.'

'London? What brings a fine man like you to Bath all the way from London?'

'I was introduced to Mr Edward's cousin in London. She said I might enjoy living in Bath and that she knew her cousin could use some help here at the hotel. She was the one who brought me here.'

'That was very kind of her.'

'She's a very nice lady. One of the finest I know.' He gave a brisk nod of his straw-coloured head for further emphasis.

'I've been admiring this garden. I cannot recall staying in a hotel or inn that serves breakfast outside like this. It's quite nice on days like today. I wonder if Mrs Edwards helped him design this. There seems to be a woman's touch about.' That was one way to find out if the man was married. The needs of his family could be a point in the negotiations.

'There is no Mrs Edwards.'

'He's not married?'

'No, sir. This was Mr Edwards's idea to serve breakfast out here. We started this last summer. I like it better than serving in the dining room. The tables are further apart out here and I don't have to worry about tripping over someone's foot.'

'Yes, I can see how that would be a concern. Well, you're doing a fine job and I'll be sure to let Mr Edwards know.'

'Thank you, sir,' he said with a beaming smile and a bow of his head, before turning to check on the next table.

That bit of information on Mr Edwards only

imagined that was what a mother would do. And he believed she would most likely be a good one.

As he rolled on to his back, the soft white sheets brushed across his bare legs. Taking a deep breath, he stared up at the blue-and-brown-striped bed hangings and wondered what kind of room Mrs Sommersby slept in. Was she still asleep or was she lying on her back right now, staring up at her own bed hangings in the way he was staring up at his?

Pushing his palms into his eyes, he rubbed away his mawkish pondering, wondering what bit of witchcraft had turned him into a schoolboy with his first taste of passion. Not that he had tasted anything of Mrs Sommersby—but every fibre of his being had wished he had. When he thought about how close he had come to kissing her last night, he let out a frustrated groan.

A desperate need for her pulsed through him and he threw his pillow across the room. Whatever it took, he was going to figure out a way to find Mrs Sommersby and when he did he was going to kiss her. He had seen the passion in her eyes. He had felt her uneven breathing on his skin. It was inevitable.

Once more he rested his head on his arm. This time instead of imagining what she was doing at that very moment, he thought more about what he would like to do to her the next time he saw her.

Less than two hours later Lane was sitting downstairs in the walled garden of The Fountain Head Hotel, drinking coffee at one of the round tables while he read the hotel's most recent edition of several newspapers. He couldn't spend all his time at the coffee house watching over Mr Sanderson's shoulder. His manager was a hardworking man and it was imperative that there was a

scratched the surface. He would try to find out more about the man from Mr Sanderson. There had to be a way to do it discreetly without revealing his plan to acquire the property. He had been trying to keep the discovery of the spring to only a very few people. The last thing he wanted was for the owner of the hotel to find out about the spring and then create a spa on their property first. The hotel had more land, they could offer more than they currently did.

His gaze dropped to the *Chronicle* that was in front of him. Could he be lucky enough to glean some additional information on Mr Edwards from the local paper?

What his eye did land on was a mention of a *'widowed Mrs S. who, Tuesday of last, had been at a ball in the Upper Assembly Rooms, speaking with a new friend, and who might be testing her famous matchmaking skills once again.'*

Thoughts of Mrs Sommersby with Miss Collingswood popped into his head. She had to be the woman they were referring to. How many widows were in town with the last initial of 'S'? Well, how many of them were fond of matchmaking—even if they didn't like to admit it? In fact, he would bet fifty pounds that she was indeed the woman who was mentioned.

He hadn't been to a ball in years. He wasn't very fond of dancing and if he wanted to play cards he could do that at his club. So why was he trying to picture her moving through the Upper Assembly Rooms with Miss Collingswood at her side in some tempting ball gown that would highlight the curves of her body and shimmer in the candlelight as she walked? He still wanted to kiss her. He still wanted to feel the soft skin of her neck while he held her there as he deepened his kiss. And he still wondered if a kiss might lead to something more.

Chapter Thirteen

As Lane walked through the gates of Sydney Gardens, he was tempted to turn around and head to the wooded space near the Royal Crescent. The muscle by his jaw started to twitch as he checked the time on his watch. It was far later than it should have been. This is what he got for spending hours daydreaming about a woman. He was already behind in his work. Today, he would only have an hour to walk through the gardens.

He took a deep breath of the clean air, taking in the smell of the expanse of grass that stretched out ahead of him that formed the bowling green. One of the things he liked best about being here was that the air smelled better in Bath than it did in London. This had been the fourth time he had walked the pathways of Sydney Gardens and he knew for certain that he would be coming back to this picturesque location each time he returned to Bath to check on his property.

Shoving his hands into the pockets of his coat, he took off at a brisk pace down one of the serpentine walks on his way to the pathway that ran alongside the canal. He strode under the leafy bowers past alcoves tucked away where one could sit on a warm day on the wooden benches. Nannies and mothers strolled past him

ing the soft fur under the dog's chin. As he did so, he looked around and tried to see if anyone was searching for it. 'You couldn't have got in here by yourself. Where's your owner?'

With small yaps, the dog appeared to try to explain.

'You've run off, haven't you? You do remind me of another dog here in Bath. Do you have a brother? Perhaps a very young uncle?'

The dog barked this time—a louder sound which carried on the breeze that was rustling the leaves on the branches above them.

'Humphrey!' The name was called out from somewhere behind him.

Lane's heart skipped a beat. 'It *is* you,' he said to the small dog that was now balancing himself up on his hind legs with his paws resting on Lane's knee. 'Tell me you have not got Mrs Sommersby caught up in some bit of shrubbery again.'

He turned his head, following the sound of her voice, but he didn't see her.

'Humphrey!' she called out again.

'He's over here!' Holding the pup firmly, he began to pat its back. 'Now you stay right where you are. Don't you try running off again until your mistress gets here. I doubt she wants to have to chase you around this park today.'

'No, she does not.'

The sound of her breathless voice behind him made him smile since there were a few times he had contemplated how she would sound after a vigorous bout of sex.

'Mr Lane!' Her eyes shifted from him and widened when she spotted her dog.

'Mrs Sommersby.'

'Oh, dear Heavens... Humphrey, what are you

thick and the sound of his heartbeat grew louder in his ears.

She licked her lips and swallowed. 'How I wish you were serious.'

'What makes you believe that I'm not?'

They were less than two feet apart. Between them, Humphrey began to wriggle in his arms and leaned out to lick Mrs Sommersby on her cheek.

'Do not think to charm me with kisses, you rascal. They have no effect on me.' But even as she said it, she reached out and rubbed the dog's little head.

From behind Mrs Sommersby he saw Miss Collingswood making her way towards them and he held up his hand in a greeting.

'Mr Lane! Imagine seeing you in this park. How did you find Humphrey?'

He gave her a friendly smile. 'He seems to have found me.' He turned back to Mrs Sommersby. 'It never occurred to me that it was him when he ran up to me. This garden is far from where I saw you walking him last.'

She lifted Humphrey out of his arms and took a step back. She even started to rock the pup in her arms the way he had seen a mother in the garden not long ago rock a fussy infant. Humphrey continued to lick her face. 'I've taken it upon myself to show Miss Collingswood more of Bath and it's a lovely place to spend a pleasant day such as this.' Her brow furrowed and she glanced quickly at her friend before meeting him in the eye. 'I've been here before. In fact, I come here often. It isn't so rare that I would be here today...with Miss Collingswood.'

'And with Humphrey.' He felt the need to add that

horrible company. 'Would you ladies care to join me during my brief walk?'

He had come here to forget her. Now, if she declined his invitation, he would be spending the remainder of his day wondering where in the garden she had gone and what she had done.

'How long do you intend to walk?' Mrs Sommersby asked, shifting her wriggling puppy in her arms.

He took out his watch from his waistcoat pocket to check. 'Another half an hour.'

As they strolled in and out of the patches of muted sunlight that shone on to the path through the leaves above them, their conversation drifted from last night's performance of *The Rivals* to the fact that she had missed her daily morning visit to the spa.

Miss Collingswood's brows drew together. 'Do you truly go every morning?'

'I do. I've been doing that for more years than I can remember.'

'But why?'

'Years ago, I went for my health. Now I suppose I go more out of habit than anything else. Bathing in the waters of the spa is wonderful. There is nothing like being submerged in all that hot water.'

Early on in her marriage she had lost a child before she could carry it to full term. She had been advised that bathing in the water could strengthen her womb, so they had moved to Bath from London and she went to the spa every day. She lost two more children after that, in much the same way as the first. After they had buried the third infant that came from her body before it was ready, Robert said that they should stop trying. He loved her too much to lose her and was afraid she would bleed out and die if it happened again. Clara had continued to go to the spa even after that in the hope that some day he might change his mind. He never did and eventually they left Bath and moved back to London. But even when she returned after he died, she still continued to bathe in the spa. Old habits were hard to break. Even those that didn't make sense any more.

'How often do you take the thermal baths?' Mr Lane asked as she stopped to let Humphrey sniff a particular tree.

'Every Tuesday and Thursday barring extenuating

thinking about her this morning, but, knowing Mr Lane, she guessed his mind was probably on business.

'Spending a late night out can truly make it hard to rise the next morning.'

Harriet's innocent comment as they strolled behind Humphrey made Mr Lane utter the funniest combination of a laugh and a cough before he caught himself and cleared his throat. Clara caught his eye and he quickly looked away. She tried to suppress a smile, knowing where his mind had gone.

Harriet slipped away from them and walked over towards a flowerbed at the side of the path and bent to smell some of the roses. Clara's eyes met his and they held for a few moments before he stepped closer to her. Their arms were almost touching. If she lifted a finger, she would be able to caress his and through her clothes it felt as if she could feel the heat radiating from his body.

Once more she imagined his mouth on hers. She wanted to kiss him. She wanted him to kiss her. And when his gaze dropped to her lips, she was thinking that maybe he wanted to kiss her, too.

The sound of two women chattering and moving around them on the gravel path was enough to break the spell and she looked over at her friend, who was still smelling the rose bushes.

'That's a Celsiana Damask rose,' she called to Harriet while she adjusted her grip on Humphrey's leash, needing something to do and say that would keep her focus away from Mr Lane's mouth.

'It's so fragrant,' Harriet replied, leaning in again to sniff it once more.

'They use the petals to make perfume.'

'I'm not surprised that you know that.' His deep voice, not far from her ear, had broken her forced con-

large thick wall of privet hedgerow that formed the outside of the maze.

'There isn't enough time.'

'We can walk with you back to the gate.' At least
Harriet wasn't pleading, which is how it probably would
have come out if Clara had said it. But when he shook
his head, it felt as if she could hardly breathe.

If she had kissed him, would he have stayed?

'That's not necessary. Enjoy the gardens, ladies.' Before either of them could reply he turned and walked
away from them with the sound of the gravel crunch-
ing under his shiny boots.

'Wait!' she called out after him rather inelegantly and
shoved Humphrey's leash into Harriet's hand.

He stopped and slowly turned around as she walked
quickly towards him. When she reached him, she realised Harriet had stayed behind.

'You offered to help me train my dog.'

A small smile was playing at the corners of his lips.
'I did, didn't I.'

'You did. I even recall you offering to do so for free.'

Raising his eyes skywards as if he was trying to recall making that offer, he folded his arms. 'Are you sure
that's what I said?'

'I am.' Their eyes met again and she was so glad
she had stopped him from walking away. 'Will you
help me?'

He shoved his hands back into his pockets and lowered his head. 'I can't.'

'Why not?'

'We want different things. It's best if we part ways.'

'What things? What do you want?'

He stepped closer. Since he was taller than she was
and they were standing so close it was as if she was al-

an eye on Humphrey so that he didn't jump out of the window from her lap. She didn't want to look at Harriet. She couldn't face the girl, knowing that Harriet liked Mr Lane.

It was Harriet who finally broke the silence that stretched between them over the sound of the rolling carriage wheels on the cobblestone streets.

'I am glad you went after him. His departure was so abrupt that it was unsettling.'

Something outside the carriage must have caught Humphrey's attention since he lifted his paws to the carriage window and let out a series of barks. 'Humphrey, shush.' He adjusted his hind legs on the jonquil fabric in her lap and barked at the window again.

'Did he explain why he needed to leave so quickly?'

'He had business to attend to.'

'And that is all?' Harriet didn't sound as if she believed her.

It had become apparent that Harriet was attracted to Mr Lane. Clara could tell that the moment they left the theatre last night when she came up with this plan on how to find him. She didn't have the heart to crush Harriet's hopes. Perhaps she should begin championing Mr Greeley.

'Why are you so quiet?' Harriet took Clara's hand in a comforting gesture that under the circumstances felt like a punch in the chest. 'I hope he didn't say anything to upset you.'

'No. He didn't.' Clara kept her eyes on Humphrey, not wanting to see Harriet's concern for her. The young woman was truly lovely and had been ignored by men who were only interested in her sister. How could Clara put her through the same pain as well?

'Please don't worry, Clara. I'm certain he likes you. I

'I am fairly certain.'

'Well, it doesn't matter. I still think you are perfect for one another.'

'I'm sure many people here in Bath would disagree.'

'I doubt Mr Lane would. When will you see him again?'

Clara shrugged with the words he whispered to her still echoing in her mind. *'The next time I see you, I'm going to kiss you.'* It would be a long time before she forgot those words.

'Do you know where he is staying?' Harriet asked. 'I thought I heard him mention The Fountain Head Hotel in town.'

'He did. You seem to have developed a habit of paying close attention to what Mr Lane says.'

'When you don't talk very much, you learn to listen well when it matters. Are you going to see him again?'

'He hasn't arranged anything, if that is what you are asking. But I do have a feeling that I will be seeing him again.'

The question was, how soon?

ing about how much he loved the way she smelled…
and talked…and would fit so perfectly in his arms if
he ever got the chance to hold her.

He needed to spend the day locked in his office,
alone, reviewing those books from the stable. But as he
walked down the dark corridor at the back of the shop
and opened the door to his office, his plans fell apart
when he spotted the Earl of Hartwick reclining back
in Lane's desk chair, with his booted feet on Lane's
large oak desk.

Lane blinked to make sure he wasn't imagining it.
'What are you doing here?'

'I would think that was fairly obvious,' Hart said,
lowering his feet and sitting forward so his forearms
were resting on the surface of the desk. 'Where the hell
have you been? It's almost noon.'

'I've been out.' Lane pointed behind him with his
thumb in the event Hart didn't know where the front
door to the coffee house was.

'Why? You never go out. I was beginning to think
you must be in a ditch somewhere with your throat
cut…probably clutching profit and loss statements with
your dying breath.' His voice was rough with anxiety
as he grabbed the papers from the desk that Lane had
intended to review today.

'Well, as you can see my throat is fine—however,
those papers aren't. If you keep crushing them in your
fist, I might have the devil of a time reading them when
you are through.'

As Hart dropped the papers on the desk, his sharp
blue eyes became hooded like a hawk. 'I looked for
that handy analysis you love to do, but didn't see it, so
I thought I'd take a crack at recalculating the numbers
myself.'

'Well, it's about time. Yes, I have news. We have come all the way from London to tell you that I have found an investor in this venture of ours.'

The weight that Lane had been carrying around in his chest was suddenly gone and he threw his head back and closed his eyes in relief. 'Thank God! Who is it? Do I know the gentleman?'

'It's Lord Musgrove.'

'I don't know anything about him.'

'Well, he didn't know anything about you either, so the field is even. He has agreed to fund this endeavour of yours, but he wants to see for himself what he will be investing in.'

'He's coming here?'

'Yes, he should arrive shortly and, if all goes as planned, we will be signing a contract with the man and getting the money we need to purchase and re-build that hotel.'

Soon, he would show Lord Musgrove just how prof-itable this spa was going to be and he would finally be able to make an offer on the hotel next door. His vision was finally going to happen.

He let out a long breath and rubbed his eyes with the palms of his hands.

'Something is different about you,' Hart commented before taking a sip from his cup. 'I can't quite put my finger on what it is, but there definitely is something different about you. Where were you this morning?'

'I told you I was out. I went for a walk in Sydney Gardens. It's this pleasure garden I discovered not far from here.'

'You were walking in a pleasure garden all this time?' He raised his cup to his lips and took a slow sip, studying Lane over the rim of porcelain. 'That's

'There isn't.'

His friends exchanged a look, which was never a good sign. His relationship with Mrs Sommersby was complicated enough. A change of subject was in order.

'Tell me about Lord Musgrove. How did you meet?'

'Andrew Pearce introduced us. So where did you meet this woman?'

'At the spa. Did Lord Musgrove indicate how much he was willing to invest?'

'Everything we need. He is interested in diversifying outside his tobacco interests. Were you bathing when you met her at the spa?'

Sarah swatted him on his shoulder.

'I'm simply trying to fill in the details so I understand how this woman could possibly bring my friend into such a state that he forgot to analyse a profit and loss statement. This is unprecedented.'

'I didn't forget.'

'Forgive me, you had better things to do.'

'No…yes…will you two leave me be so I can look at these figures in peace?'

'Come with me, Sarah. We will leave Lane to pretend he is working when we know he will be pining for his…oh, what was the word?'

'His friend,' Sarah replied with a laugh.

'Oh, yes, his friend. I will inform you when Lord Musgrove arrives. In the meantime, we are staying with Lyonsdale at Number Twelve on the Royal Crescent. Send word to his home if you need anything.'

What he needed was Mrs Sommersby. He couldn't call on her. He didn't know where she lived. If he wanted to see her again, he would have to go to a place he knew she would be. When they met at the park by the Crescent that day, she had mentioned various entertain-

Chapter Sixteen

Clara stood on the edge of the dance floor in the large ballroom of the Upper Assembly Rooms with the Dowager Duchess watching Harriet fade into the woodwork as her sister Ann took centre stage among a group of young gentlemen.

She looked over at the Dowager standing beside her and tried not to frown. 'I thought you were going to invite Mr Greeley this evening.'

'The man was called out of town on a family matter.'

'Well, that's unfortunate. If she wasn't an unmarried young woman, I'd take her with me into the card room.'

'If she wasn't an unmarried woman, you wouldn't have to. And where is your Mr Lane this evening?'

'He is not *my* Mr Lane and I have no idea.' She hadn't seen or heard from him for days and was beginning to wonder if he, too, had been called out of town.

'Pity. There was something about that man I liked.'

There was a lot about him that she had liked as well—more than she would care to admit, even to herself. She couldn't trust herself when it came to men. She had married for love and it had turned into a disaster. It was probably smarter to keep her distance from him anyway.

the city frequently had become a friend. He made his way through the crowd to her, looking completely un-ruffled in his impeccable evening attire.

'I didn't know you had returned from London.'

He rose from his bow with a sparkle in his grey-blue eyes. 'If I knew you would be missing me that much, I would have called on you directly after we crossed the river.'

'I always miss you when you are gone. I become completely despondent. It is remarked upon by all who see me and is written about extensively in the *Chronicle*,' she replied with excessive dramatic inflection and let out a long sigh.

'I've told you there is a remedy for that, but you refuse to marry me, so it appears, until you do, you will find your name in the papers with some regularity.'

Shaking out her fan, she hid her smile from him, but knew by his expression that he saw the merriment in her eyes. Glancing at the Dowager, she saw Eleanor was watching their exchange with marked attention. 'Your Grace, may I introduce you to Mr Charles Whelby? Mr Whelby is a friend and terrible tease. Mr Whelby, may I present Eleanor, the Dowager Duchess of Lyonsdale?'

'Your Grace, it is an honour to make your acquaintance.' In the candlelight from the five enormous cut-glass chandeliers hanging high above the room, the small diamond stickpin in his cravat winked at them as he bowed.

'Did I hear you have recently come from London, sir?'

'I have, Your Grace.'

'I am quite fond of London and spend most of the year there myself. Most people my age prefer the countryside. I find no comfort in being left with such a restricted number of companions.'

'He had come down with a particularly bad cold and wanted someone to nurse him back to health.'

'As a wife would do,' he explained in his defence, adjusting the cuff on his impeccably cut tailcoat with his head bent down so all she could see was his very close-cropped brown hair that was just starting to turn grey.

'Well, since you will not be marrying Mrs Sommersby, perhaps we might interest you in meeting another lady?'

'She is not a fine pair of embroidered gloves that you can offer like that,' Clara said, chastising her outspoken friend.

The Dowager waved her pink-gloved hand at her. 'I didn't say that she was—however, I find being direct is the best course of action. This way no one can misconstrue your meaning.'

'I don't believe anyone could ever misconstrue your meaning.'

'Which has served me well in life and why I am so good at determining which people should be together.' She turned her attention back to Charles. 'Mr Whelby, if you would care to meet a lovely young woman who is in attendance tonight, please let me know.'

'I will, should I decide to expand my social circle.' Once more he seemed amused by the Dowager's directness. It was amazing that he hadn't made an excuse to run away by now.

'Capital. Please do. Now, if you will both excuse me, I think I will go and save that girl from boredom.' She walked slowly away from them towards Harriet. Clara couldn't imagine what the woman did to relieve boredom in a ballroom and she wasn't certain it would be good for her to find out.

'What a very unusual woman,' Charles said, follow-

what was being discussed, she would join in, instead of standing back the way she is.'

It wasn't that easy. She knew that from experience. She knew what it was like to stand beside a sister that men wanted and they barely noticed you at all, even though you were less than two feet from her. She knew what it was like when you tried to join in a conversation and the people around you didn't even acknowledge what you said. It was as though you were invisible. Eventually you stopped contributing. Being invisible was so much easier on your soul when you were the one who decided it was how you wanted to be.

Charles's attention remained on the little group. 'Who are they?'

'They are the Collingswood sisters. Their family is leasing the house next door.'

'On the Crescent?' His brows rose as he nodded his head in approval of the fashionable address. 'They must have deep pockets. What of the father?'

'He is a barrister who has presented his cases before Parliament and the son of a baron.'

Charles was casting an appraising gaze over Harriet and Ann. 'Neither are spoken for?'

'No. I know the blonde has had numerous offers, but has not found a gentleman that suits her fancy.'

His eyes remained on the small party a bit longer before finally returning his attention to Clara. 'Well, we could stand here for the rest of the night watching your friend, or we could dance. I think we should dance.'

Since the Dowager was going over to Harriet, Clara was certain she would find a way to make the girl feel appreciated. She looked back up at Charles. 'Are you asking me to dance?'

'Would you like me to?'

They separated once again.

'Well, let's see. I've been reading all my correspondence that has piled up on my desk. Oh, and I had breakfast in the garden at The Fountain Head while I met with your cousin, Phillip.' Charles was one of only a small handful of people who knew she owned the hotel. 'Apparently, more and more people from Bath have taken to having breakfast in the garden lately. Friends are telling friends. Which is good news for the owner.'

'I'm sure the owner is quite pleased. Did you enjoy their new offerings for breakfast?' she asked as he came up once again at her side.

'There wasn't anything that was new since the last time I was there.'

They separated once more and anger started to rise up inside her. She had specifically told Phillip she wanted to expand the menu and he had agreed he would. It was times like this when she regretted having her cousin manage the establishment. Perhaps if they weren't related she would have a manager who did not see fit to go against her wishes.

'You are certain?'

'Yes. It was the usual fare of Sally Lunn buns and bread.'

She wanted to storm off the dance floor and go over to The Fountain Head to demand to know why he had disregarded her request. As it stood, she was now dancing with her hands balled into two fists. Why was it so difficult for a man to realise that she knew what she was doing?

Clara stared off into the distance as she shouted things at Phillip in her head that no lady should ever say out loud. Then she caught the eye of a gentleman

Chapter Seventeen

She was in green satin. Lane had wondered what colour Mrs Sommersby would be wearing on his walk over to the Upper Assembly Rooms. What someone was going to wear had never been any of his concern before, but tonight he kept trying to imagine what colour silk or satin would be against her skin.

When he entered the building, he was hoping he wouldn't find her in the ballroom. It would have been easier if she were in the card room. No one danced in there and he was fairly skilled at cards. But when he spied her on the dance floor with the impeccably groomed, middle-aged gentleman, he was not surprised. Mrs Sommersby would indeed be a woman who danced. And once he spotted her, he didn't want to look away.

The desire to kiss her deeply and passionately while holding her in his arms had not diminished. If anything, in that gown and under the glow of the candlelight, he wanted her even more.

How she managed to spot him in the middle of the dance was a mystery. Lane thought he had blended in completely with every other man in the room dressed in fine black evening wear. Yet somehow during one par-

thing intense flared between them and he didn't miss when her tongue peeked out and briefly touched the dip in her top lip.

He wanted to taste that lip and the plump one below it. He wanted to savour the feel of her lips against his and slide his tongue over hers to see how she would respond. Two gentlemen came around from behind him and blocked Lane's view of her as they walked in her direction.

When she came back into view, she was standing in the very spot she had been in, looking stunning in her green-satin gown with her white-silk gloves that had fallen below her elbows. But now she was all alone. The gentleman she had been dancing with was no longer by her side. Whether it was intentional or not, he couldn't tell, but her gaze slid slowly down his body and it became impossible to swallow.

This was it. She was all alone now. This was what he had come here for.

He approached her slowly, holding her gaze and thinking that she might disappear back into the crowd if he rushed this. When he was less than three feet from her, Mrs Sommersby's gaze dropped to his mouth. Did she want him to drag her out of the assembly?

'Mr Lane.' Her voice was smooth like fine brandy and it had the ability to stir his soul with just the sound of his name. As she dipped into a shallow curtsy and lowered her head, he had the perfect view of the smooth, tempting skin of the upper swells of her shapely breasts and had to rub his gloved fingers across his palm to quell the itch to touch her.

'Good evening, Mrs Sommersby.' It came out surprisingly composed considering the inner turmoil he

'I find there is something in this room that interests me very much.'

She looked up at him from the corner of her eye. 'Something?'

'Someone.'

'Ah, I see. You seemed to have disappeared from the streets of Bath as of late. I thought you had left town. I was disappointed we hadn't had the chance to say goodbye.'

'I've been consumed with work.'

'Your investments.'

'Yes. Success only comes from long hours and dedication.'

There were four tiers of benches that lined the outer portion of the room and she headed towards them.

'And you're successful?'

'Very.'

'It hasn't escaped my notice how committed you are to your work.'

With her hand, she gestured towards the empty seats at the end of the second tier. 'Shall we?'

He might get a reprieve from dancing after all. Nodding his agreement, he waited for her to sit and then took the end seat beside her. She pushed the wrinkles out of her skirt and he couldn't help notice her thighs were outlined in green satin that shimmered in the candlelight.

The movement of her hand as she opened her fan broke his concentration.

'It feels nice to sit down. This is the first time I have taken a seat all night. One of the advantages of my age is that I do not need to stand about waiting to be seen.'

'You make it sound as if we have one foot in the grave.'

'*We* don't. But I am far closer to it than you are.' She

spread from her body to him. She must have felt it, too, since she glanced at the area where their bodies were touching.

'Now that I have cured your desire,' she whispered to him behind her fan, 'please don't feel obliged to remain here with me. I understand.'

'That has changed nothing. If anything, sitting this close to you while you are in that gown has made me want to kiss you even more. And make no mistake, Mrs Sommersby—I will be kissing you some time tonight.'

Her eyes flew to his and then dropped to his lips. What he wouldn't give to kiss her right now.

'But how could you still want to? I am so much older than you.'

'You are not that much older and, in addition, you telling me your age has not changed anything about you. You are still the most captivating woman I know.'

'Then you must know very few women.'

'Do not do that. Do not try to diminish yourself to me. I will draw my own conclusions about you.'

'By the flattering glow of candlelight, you may think you have not changed your mind. But when the sun comes up, you will find you see a different portrait.'

'You truly have no idea how much I wish I could kiss you now and prove you wrong.'

Her breath caught. He heard it. And it gave him immense satisfaction.

As if to give herself time to regain her composure, she looked away from him and out into the crowd. Eventually her gaze settled on a small group of young dandies that were surrounding a tall, thin blonde woman whose hair was woven with a pale pink ribbon in it. He couldn't understand why this particular group had captured Mrs Sommersby's interest, until he spotted Miss

'I have no brothers or sisters,' he replied. 'And you?'

'I have an older sister.' Her eyes remained on Miss Collingswood's party. 'Mary was always the prettier one. She was always very comfortable conversing in crowds. I was not.' Their eyes met briefly and he sensed a sad nostalgic wave come over her. She adjusted her seat on the bench and looked back out at her young friend.

'I find it hard to believe that you are not accomplished in conversing in a crowd. And I also believe it isn't possible that your sister is prettier than you.'

'You flatter me again, sir.' She gifted him with a smile that shone in her eyes. 'Over the years it became easier to speak in groups of people. It happened after I married my husband, God rest his soul. But even now, I actually prefer smaller intimate groups of people I am well acquainted with than standing in a group with virtual strangers. I suppose I have become skilled at hiding that part of me from the world.'

Miss Collingswood looked sad. Everyone was laughing at something her sister had said, but Miss Collingswood looked lost in her own thoughts. No one seemed to notice. No one seemed to even see her standing there.

'I know what it is like to be ignored,' he said. 'To feel as though you don't quite have a place in the room. As though maybe your place isn't even in the room.'

He wasn't sure why he had admitted that to her. He never liked to think about what it felt like to be a bastard.

She reached out and squeezed his hand that was resting on his thigh. 'There are occasions when people can be so thoughtless.'

'That was really very kind of you to ask me to dance. I was hoping that Mr Greeley would be here tonight, but the Dowager said that she heard he'd had to go out of town to Plymouth to tend to a family matter. Not that I am not grateful that you have asked me to dance. I just thought I'd mention Mr Greeley…and my interest in him.'

'Uh-huh.'

'You never did say if you have seen Mrs Sommersby. She is here in a lovely green gown. It is very pretty and she looks so beautiful in it. I'm certain if you look around for her, you will find her. She is such wonderful company.'

'Uh-huh.'

'What are you doing, Mr Lane?'

'Remembering the sequence.'

'Of what?'

'The steps.'

They parted ways and he followed the gentleman on his right side as he walked around his particular group of four dancers.

'You don't know the minuet?'

'I haven't danced it in a long time.'

'Yet you decided to dance it with me?'

'My apologies for being a less-than-adequate partner.'

'Oh, Mr Lane, I think you are the finest partner I have ever had.' There was a brief shimmer of unshed tears in her eyes before she very quietly instructed him on the movements just low enough so only he could hear her.

to his advantage in the cut of his well-made clothing. And through his white stockings she could see a pair of very nice, very defined calf muscles.

'He does seem to be concentrating quite a bit,' the Dowager observed in a low voice.

'I wonder what she is saying that he finds so interesting?'

'Perhaps she is talking about you.'

Clara eyed her friend. 'I don't know why he would find anything about me interesting? I am much too old for him.'

'I doubt Mr Lane feels you are. The two of you have a way when you are together. One gets the sense that in a room full of people, the two of you feel as though you are all alone.'

'What does that even mean?'

'It means that I have watched you at the theatre and tonight sitting here on the benches. You have some type of connection to one another. It's not something I see frequently. It's not something one can manufacture. It comes from somewhere in the soul.'

'Eleanor, have you been reading poetry again?'

The Dowager waved her gloved hand at Clara and the diamonds in her bracelet sparkled. 'That does not signify. I know what I see. I have been at this far too long to miss something as blatant as this.'

'And what is it that you have been at?'

'Why, matchmaking.'

'We are not a match. I am old enough to be his... young aunt.'

'Has it escaped your notice that I am the champion of unlikely matches? Just look at my grandson and his American wife. No other duke had ever married an American before. There was quite a to-do about his

don. I introduced them the night I took Harriet to the theatre.'

'London. Well, that is something.'

By the slightly crestfallen look in her eyes, Clara could tell she was disappointed that Mr Lane was not in possession of a title.

'I assume by the look of him and his manners that he is from a respectable part of town.'

Clara had no idea where in London he lived. It had never come up in their discussions and the one time Harriet had brought up London when they were sitting having breakfast, he had left after barely acknowledging her comment. She also knew nothing of his family save for the fact that he had no brothers or sisters. For someone who had intended to arrange a match between the man and this woman's daughter, she truly had been remiss in finding out the necessary details to determine if he would have been a respectable match for the girl. But based on his character, she was certain he would check off all the other necessary points on her list.

'Will he be in Bath for long?'

'I am not sure how much longer he is to remain. He is here on a business matter.'

Mrs Collingswood turned to look at the dance floor once more. 'A businessman. What kind?'

'A respectable one.' At least she hoped he was. What had they been talking about each time they were together that she didn't know the answer to this?

The vague response seemed to perplex Mrs Collingswood, but she didn't press and once more she looked back at her daughter and Mr Lane. 'Well, at least she is on the dance floor. Thank you for arranging this.'

'Harriet is a dear girl. That dance was not done at my prompting.'

her unique charms. And now you have introduced her to Mr Lane. I would assume being a friend of yours that he is from a good family. One can tell he is in possession of a good fortune by the cut of his clothes.'

There was no sense in getting this woman's hopes up about Mr Lane and she might be able to save Harriet from being nagged by her mother about him if she could set the record straight. 'From what we can tell, they are only sharing one dance. You may find there are other gentlemen here in Bath who appreciate Harriet's charms and fine character. In fact, I am fairly certain of it.'

'I agree,' Eleanor said. 'There are other gentlemen closer to her own age who I have noticed have shown an interest in her.'

Mrs Collingswood looked sceptical. 'With all due respect, Your Grace, I shall believe that when I see it with my own eyes. Perhaps Mr King might know more about Mr Lane. As the Master of Ceremonies here, he does make it his business to know about everyone who comes to Bath.'

Just then the dance ended and Mr Lane returned Harriet to the vacant area of the ballroom where earlier her sister had been entertaining all those young men. Apparently Mr Ross had got up the courage to ask Ann to dance, because in a few short minutes they joined the couple and Harriet was extending introductions. Like a bee seeking some nectar, Mrs Collingswood excused herself rather quickly and made her way through the crowd to Harriet for her own introduction to Mr Lane.

The Dowager's gaze followed her as she approached the small group. 'That poor, dear girl.'

'Do you see why I have been avoiding them? That woman makes my head ache.'

Was Mr Lane going to run? Is this how their evening would end?

Eleanor nudged her arm with her pointy elbow. 'Ah, there is just something about a bachelor of a certain age,' she observed with amusement in her voice. 'They do become experts in extricating themselves from situations with matchmaking mothers.'

Mr Lane wasn't leaving. At least not yet. He was striding towards them in a purposeful manner.

Eleanor stood and adjusted her reticule on her wrist. 'That didn't take very long at all. Well, I see an old friend across the room. Do give Mr Lane my best and if, by some chance, I do not see you for the remainder of the ball, do have a lovely evening.'

'I'm sure you will see me. I always stay to the end.'

'I'm not so sure about that.' And with that, Eleanor left her to face Mr Lane alone.

The sight of him with his eyes locked on hers, stalking across the room, was stirring a heat inside her. From the look on his face he appeared to either want to grab her in his arms and kiss her, or ring a peel over her for pushing Mrs Collingswood in his direction. She was fervently hoping it was the former. Snapping open her fan, she attempted to cool any flush of passion that might be ready to colour her cheeks at the thought of it.

Eleanor was correct in her assessment of him. Mr Lane did not appear to have any qualms about expertly excusing himself from situations he did not want to be in. She had experienced that first hand on a number of occasions. The question was, would he be doing it again when he reached her? Was he just going to bid her a goodnight and leave out of exasperation?

The minute he reached her there was a palpable in-

the ballroom, across the corridor and into the vestibule outside the cloakroom where two liveried attendants were there ready to take the coats, hats and walking sticks of the people attending the ball. No one else was about.

This did not constitute being alone in Clara's eyes. The two attendants were right there and people could enter the area at any moment. However, just as she was about to point that out to Mr Lane, he walked up to one of the attendants and whispered something to him while he placed something in the man's hand.

While he strode back to Clara, the intensity of his gaze bore into her sending butterflies around her stomach. Before she was able to ask him what he had said to the man, he pulled her by her hand through the doorway that was a few feet away on her right and closed the white panelled door behind them. The small room he dragged her into was painted a celery green and was lit by four sconces on the wall. Tables lined the walls with stacks of coats and beaver hats and walking sticks on them. They were in the actual cloakroom. In all the years she had been coming to this building she had never seen this room before since only the attendants ever went in here.

She opened her mouth to once more explain her innocence to him, when he suddenly wrapped his arm around her waist and pulled her up against his hard chest. His hand rested in the small of her back and the tips of his fingers skimmed the top of her bottom. If she took a deep breath, which was currently impossible surrounded by all his masculinity, he would know because her breasts would press even further against him. Instinctively her hands went to his shoulders and then moved down to curve around his biceps. If he let go of

'Where shall we go?' she asked, closing the jewelled clasp on her cloak while he adjusted the brim of his hat.

'We could take my carriage to Sydney Gardens to watch the fireworks.'

She shook her head and a small smile lifted the corners to those lips that he was dying to taste again. 'I don't think it would be wise to be alone in a carriage with you right now.'

'And why would that be unwise?' He eyed her profile as she began to walk beside him down the darkened empty street.

'Because you, Mr Lane, are far too tempting.'

'I'm too tempting? You're the one who made it imperative that I find a secluded spot in that building so I could finally kiss you.'

They turned right on the pavement and began heading slowly down the deserted street.

'So where shall we go?' he asked after they walked in silence for a bit.

She gave a slight lift of her shoulder. 'Suppose we walk aimlessly all night long and simply arrive back at where we started?'

Lane stopped and stepped in front of her. She appeared to study him intently.

'I think we can both agree, we are far from where we started already. We are going somewhere. Why don't you tell me where?'

'We have just started out on this journey. I think it is too soon to tell.' Her voice faded in the hushed stillness.

There was something about talking with her that made him smile. She had a quick mind and it was one of the many things he was finding that he liked about her. 'Fair enough. I shall let you take the lead.' He held

Chapter Nineteen

After all this time, Lane finally had her in his arms—and he wasn't going to let her go. Lowering his head for that final inch, he claimed her lips with a hungry kiss.

It was as if he had spent weeks in the desert and she was his last drop of water. He wanted to savour every moment of the feel of her soft lips against his and the way her body melted into his. She kissed him back with a passion that belied her normal refined demeanour. It surprised him for a second before he lifted her up, spun her around and pressed her back against the door—all the while never breaking their kiss.

She was clutching him with her fingers digging into his arms. He spread his legs and pushed his hand into the small of her lower back bringing her against his very hard length. There was no way to tell if the movement of her lower abdomen against him was intentional or instinctual. He wasn't about to stop kissing her to ask.

The need for her was becoming too strong and he let out a low guttural groan. The only place he could lay her down was on top of a pile of coats and he struggled with the notion of stopping their kiss to move them

his arm out to her and they strolled on the street known as the King's Circus.

This circular area in town had a round centre-gated garden surrounded by terraced town houses that gave the appearance of one long building. In the dark of the night with the warm lights coming from the buildings, it somehow felt as if they had stepped into a private haven. The roads were deserted at this hour with people already settled into their various evening entertainments. They were free to walk together without curious eyes upon them. However, Lane knew that could change at any moment. If only they could find somewhere completely private. As he looked over at her, he took note that she was very quiet, almost lost in thought, and he remembered seeing her on the dance floor with that well-dressed gentleman and how he sensed the man had angered her towards the end of the dance. Could she be thinking about that now?

'Do you mind if I ask you a question?'

The sound of his voice seemed to bring her out of her musings and she shook her head.

'Tonight, I spotted you on the dance floor with another gentleman. While you were dancing it appeared that he said something to upset you. What did he say?'

He was prepared for anything she was going to tell him, because no matter what it was he was going to find the man after their walk and make him apologise to her. He might even need to beat him to a pulp, depending on what he said.

She let out a sigh. 'It is nothing that you would understand.'

His mind raced with inappropriate scenarios. 'Why don't you tell me anyway?'

'There are times being a woman can be very trying.

have them go against your wishes or you will find someone else to handle your affairs. Let him see your anger.'

'Why are you not telling me that I should listen to
him? That he must know more than I do about these
things because he is a man?'

'Because I believe you are smart enough to know
sound advice when you hear it and would not place any
investment in danger due to vanity.'

'You can tell that about me?'

'I can.'

'If I show my anger, he will accuse me of being a
hysterical female. That is why when I am angry with
him I typically write him a letter.'

'Are you planning on sobbing and throwing yourself on the floor?'

She stopped walking, appearing highly insulted. 'Of
course not.'

'Then let him experience your anger. Do not hesitate. Show him you are strong in your convictions and
will not tolerate his interference.'

They turned on to the pavement that led to the Royal
Crescent. This was where Hart was staying and where
Lyonsdale was. He scanned the long row of thirty pale
stone terraced houses that made up this curved row and
tried to recall which one his friends were in.

'Well, I suppose there is no reason for me to return
to the Assembly Rooms now,' she said, as she watched
him search out the windows that were lit by the yellow
glow of candlelight. 'I live over there.' She pointed to
the fifth door.

Well, she must have been very good with her investments if she could afford to live here.

'What of your carriage?'

'As you can see, I am not far from the Assembly

ter and was making her body hot with the need to kiss him again. Their brief time in the cloakroom was just long enough to make her crave the feel of his lips on hers once more—or all night long.

She had only been with one man in her life and that was Robert. Now, every piece of her wanted to be with Lane. That thought was both exciting and terrifying. It was exciting to imagine what it would be like to roll around the sheets with him and it was a delicious sensation to savour. And she would have, except part of her was terrified to trust her heart again. She knew it was easy to fall for someone who was all wrong for you. Perhaps Lane was all wrong for her? She wouldn't marry him, so where would this lead?

The sound of muted barking came through the window near them and a rapid soft pounding could be heard. It was Humphrey, who must have been standing up on the window seat, barking excitedly at Lane. Her wonderful puppy gave her something to focus on that did not have to do with her soft bed and Lane's amazing kisses. Her old butler, Darby, came to the window, wearing his dark coat and dark stock around his neck. He picked up Humphrey in his white-gloved hands and caught her eye through the wavy glass. She gave him a slight nod and a small smile. The man glanced at Lane before disappearing into the room.

'Thank you again for walking me home.' She took a step towards the door and removed a key from her reticule.

'It was my pleasure. I take it this is goodnight, then.' He was waiting to see if she was going to invite him in and she wished with every fibre of her being that she could. But her staff was still up and her neighbours

When Lane released his hold on Humphrey and stood up, her dog barked up at him. But when Lane shushed him, the dog immediately quietened down. How was it that he had spent such little time with her dog and had made more progress with him than she or anyone of her staff had?

'Madam, if I may. This gentleman might be of some assistance.'

This would be a perfect way to see him during respectable hours and she really could use the help with Humphrey. 'Would you have some time tomorrow to work with him?'

'I could be here by two.'

Inside, she was bursting with excitement at the notion she would be able to spend time alone with him tomorrow. However, on the outside she tried to remain calm and composed. 'I will see you then.'

There was a flash of something in his eyes. Was he feeling the same way?

'And thank you for your advice earlier. I will forgo my letter-writing this time.'

'Excellent. You will feel much better afterwards. I assure you.'

Humphrey dropped his head down to rest on Lane's foot.

'My dog really does like you.'

'I'd say he has excellent taste,' he replied, appearing rather pleased with himself.

The moment standing there at her door with him and her dog had an indefinable feeling of rightness about it. With her back to the door she had no way to know where Darby had gone. If she was certain he was not standing within eyesight of her, she would have reached over and pulled Lane in for a kiss.

And what she had forgotten was for a way to kiss him goodnight inside her home away from the eyes of the neighbours and her staff.

Her entire body leaned into his as she wrapped her arms around his neck and pulled him in for a deep kiss. Within seconds his warm hands were cradling her waist and her hands were cupping his cheeks, needing to feel his bare skin. When they finally separated, he seemed pleasantly surprised by her boldness.

'I just wanted to kiss you goodnight,' she said, feeling the need to explain her actions as she placed her hand on the door handle.

'I'm glad you did. You gave me more to think about when I go to bed tonight. Sweet dreams, Clara.' His pleasure at this unexpected end to the evening shone in his eyes before he walked out of the door when she opened it for him.

'What type of proposition?'

'Well, as you are aware I have purchased the coffee house next door and I've thought about the possibility of expanding the business. I cannot expand south since the church is there and I was wondering if you would consider selling your hotel?'

Mr Edwards blinked a few times as if he wasn't sure if he had heard Lane correctly. 'We... I... I am not interested in selling.'

'I realise that your hotel must do very well—however, I am prepared to offer you a substantial amount of money for it.'

'That is very generous of you, Mr Lane, however, as I said I will not sell this hotel.'

'But don't you want to even know the amount I am willing to offer you for it?'

There was a marked hesitation in his movement before he pressed his thumb along the surface of his large oak partners' desk and moved his gaze away from Lane. 'If you would like to present your offer I would be happy to oblige you by reviewing it. However, you should know that I will never sell this hotel.'

He said that now, but he didn't know how high Lane was willing to go with his offer. He took a piece of paper out of his waistcoat with the generous offer in writing and slid it across the table to Mr Edwards.

The man's eyes opened wider than Lane had ever seen them go as he glanced down at the paper. He swallowed hard and once more he refolded his arms. 'I am sorry, but as I stated before the hotel is not for sale.'

Lane took the paper back and crossed out the amount he was willing to offer and wrote a higher amount down. He was prepared to negotiate with the man. In fact, he expected it.

thinking she would ever be kissed again, ages ago. But ever since he'd helped her out of the shrubbery and their lips had been mere inches apart, she found she had thought about kissing him a few times each day. And now that she actually knew what it felt like to have his lips against hers, she knew she was going to have a hard time *not* thinking about it—and thinking about it made her practically giddy. That was completely out of character for her. While she did enjoy finding humour in a situation, no one of her acquaintance would ever accuse her of being giddy. She wasn't even giddy when she was Harriet's age.

When she finally did get out of bed she realised that if she didn't find a way to occupy herself until Lane arrived at two o'clock, she would go mad. She decided to take his advice and go to see Phillip and find out why he had disregarded her direction to change the menu at the hotel.

By half past eight she was waiting for him in his office at the hotel and when he walked in, she could see by the look in his eye he wasn't at all happy to see her at such an early hour.

'Why did you lie to me and tell me that you would adjust the breakfast menu?'

She was familiar with that placating look he started to give her and he opened his mouth to reply, but she held up her hand. 'Never you mind. I don't want your excuses.'

Because of her diminutive stature, she never liked to have important discussions with Phillip when she was standing up. It felt as if her height reinforced the opinion that she was a delicate woman who needed to be protected from the world. She was no delicate creature.

never consider selling it when they discussed his concerns that, if she did, he would be out of a job. Now she had let him know that just because she would not be selling the hotel it did not mean that his job would be secure no matter his actions. And thanks to Lane she had the satisfaction of seeing how her words had affected him. It was glorious! She had even received a note from Phillip later that morning, but she decided to wait until after Lane left to read what she assumed was a letter of apology from the man.

Now, as she watched for Lane on the window seat of her sun-drenched drawing room that overlooked the front of the Crescent, she was practically bubbling with her eagerness to tell him that she had taken his bit of brilliant advice and it had felt wonderful to do so. But when Darby had finally escorted Lane into the room at fifteen minutes past the hour it might have been in her best interest to offer him a glass of brandy or ale before she told him about her morning. While she had been having a wonderful day, it appeared that he had not.

His brow was all furrowed and his movements were stiff as he bowed his greeting to her as she stood. Clara had arranged for tea to be brought up when Lane had arrived, but now she wasn't certain if he planned to stay long enough to have a cup. Darby, on the other hand, looked as if he was trying his best to contain his pleasure that the man was here to help them deal with her small but energetic puppy.

'I do appreciate you coming here today to help me with Humphrey, but I know you are here in Bath for business. Please do not feel as if you are under any obligation to stay should you have other things that require your attention.' How she wished he would stay.

'I beg to differ.'

He leaned forward and met her in a kiss. She had been hoping all day that he would kiss her again and she was contemplating kissing him first. The feel of his lips on hers sent a delicious sensation through her body and it didn't take long before she opened to him completely. Within seconds of deepening the kiss, she wrapped her arms around his neck and savoured the feel of his warm hands on her back and the silken waves of his thick blond hair against her fingers.

When he pulled his head back there was a devilish look in his eyes. 'Now that was better than tea.'

It warmed her heart to see him smile again.

'My mother always said that a good cup of tea can fix anything. There is magic in tea.'

With his warm fingers, he pushed away a tendril of hair by her neck, caressing her skin as he went. 'There was magic in that kiss.' As if to prove his point, he leaned forward and planted a provocative kiss on the hollow of her neck.

There was magic there because even though his lips were on a small spot on her neck, she felt his touch throughout her body. 'I thought you were here to train my dog,' she was just able to utter breathlessly.

He continued to trace a line of kisses along her neck. 'We can call this anything you like.'

His teasing comment made her laugh. What she *would* like would be for him to lay her down on the sofa and kiss the rest of her. Whatever he was doing to her neck had her imagining him doing it while he was lying on top of her with nothing between them. She could practically feel his bare skin against hers. She could just imagine what it would feel like to have him inside her. Just as Lane's hand settled on her breast,

'I am simply rubbing his back.'

'On the sofa.'

'Well, that is where we are sitting.'

'He doesn't belong on the sofa. The sofa is for humans. The floor is for a dog.'

'But we cuddle up here.'

'Then cuddle with him down there.'

'On the floor?' *He was mad.*

'If you want him to understand that he needs to defer to you, you have to show him that you have certain privileges in this house that he does not. What else do you allow him to climb on? Do you allow him to sit at the dining-room table with you?'

'Of course not.'

'Do you let him crawl into bed with you?'

They were cosy that way. She liked how he would snuggle up beside her and rest his head under her chin while he fell asleep.

'You do, don't you?'

'What I do in my bed at night is of no concern of yours.' But deep down she wished it were.

'You do.' He let out a sigh. 'You must show him that you are the head of this household. You cannot do that if you are sleeping in the same bed.'

She picked Humphrey up and placed him on her lap to cuddle with him. 'Where is he supposed to sleep? And do not say the floor. It is much too hard down there for him to sleep there all night long.'

'You can arrange a cushion for him.'

'It's not the same.' Apparently, Humphrey agreed because he let out a series of barks.

'Do you want me to truly train him or did you just want me here to kiss me?' The teasing sound was back in his voice.

Chapter Twenty-One

'How in the world did I allow you to talk me into this?' she asked, following him outside her front door. 'This is not a good idea.'

Lane could tell by the look on Clara's face that she was intrigued and terrified at the same time. They stood on the pavement in front of her home between the iron gates with Humphrey beside them without his leash. He was wagging his tail and looking up between them. Already he was able to understand that he could not run off and he needed to watch them for permission. Lane prayed there were no squirrels nearby. If there were, there was no telling how long he would find himself chasing Humphrey this afternoon.

'Whenever you are ready,' he said to Clara.

They turned out of her gate to the right and started to stroll along the Crescent to begin their short walk. There was no sense in keeping Humphrey out for a long time without his leash. It was too risky. They would just walk along for a bit to see if the dog would obey before taking him back home.

'Come, Humphrey,' she called out and the dog padded over to her side and then circled around to walk between them.

turned to him and broke the silence that had surrounded them for the last ten minutes.

'I will miss you when you are gone.'

It was a short statement—just eight words. But those words had hit him in the chest and meant so much. He wanted to say it back to her. He wanted to admit that he was not looking forward to the days when he would wake in the morning without a sense of anticipation that he might see her somewhere. His days would be darker without Clara in them. She had every right to expect him to say it back—and yet he couldn't.

Growing up in the Foundling Hospital had taught him at a very early age that children could be cruel and that admitting your feelings left you vulnerable. Those two things had proved to be a devastating combination. Life was safer on your soul if you kept your feelings to yourself.

Their eyes met and held for several heartbeats. She was waiting for him to say it back to her. It was in her eyes.

Humphrey let out a series of barks, breaking into this moment that was crushing his chest. While it first appeared that Humphrey was barking up at them, he was in fact barking at the expensively outfitted landau with an official crest on its door that was parked in front of Clara's home and at the footmen wearing the burgundy livery of Clara's staff who were unloading trunks from it and bringing them inside her house. As if she could sense Humphrey's excitement at all the commotion, Clara picked him up and cradled him in her arms as they walked forward.

'Were you expecting guests?'

'No, but my nieces do have a habit of showing up unannounced. It might be one thing we Sommersby

'You are too loud,' he said, picking the puppy up. He told himself he did it to ensure Humphrey didn't run over and paw at the women for attention. But he also took some comfort in holding the warm little dog that snuggled into the crook of his arm.

You knew your feelings ran deep when you would also miss her dog when you left.

When he looked back over at the women all four of them were staring at him.

'That dog looks like Ambrose,' the youngest one commented offhandedly, stepping back from Clara.

There was an apologetic look in Clara's eyes as she looked directly at him. 'It is Ambrose.'

'But this gentleman called him Humphrey.'

'It's a long story.'

'They always are,' the one with the finest clothes and the sapphire necklace said, eyeing him openly.

The younger one gave him a friendly smile and then turned to Clara. 'Is this gentleman a friend of yours?'

They were friends, he supposed…by definition. But he'd never had a friend whom he'd kissed before. He'd certainly never had a friend who he'd wanted desperately to bed—countless times.

The woman waited for a response and continued to glance expectantly between him and Clara. Humphrey took this opportunity to lick his chin as if to inform the woman that Lane was his friend as well.

Clara walked over and guided him by the arm closer to the woman as if she realised it would be better if they were introduced to each other without the entire Crescent having to hear the conversation. 'He is. Mr Lane, may I introduce my nieces to you. This is Elizabeth, the Duchess of Skeffington,' she said, gesturing to the one

The Duchess began walking through the opening of the black wrought-iron gates that led to Clara's front door and lifted the skirt of her purple gown to take the step. 'You always have the best tea. It's just what I need after that ride.'

He put Humphrey down and was just about to shoo him into the house and take his leave to return back to the coffee house when Lady Juliet called out, 'Isn't Mr Lane going to join us?'

'Oh, please do, Mr Lane,' Lady Charlotte added. 'We did not mean to impose on your visit with our aunt.'

To hear Lady Charlotte refer to Clara as her aunt was strange to his ears. He didn't think of Clara as anyone's aunt. He didn't think of Clara as being related to anyone. 'I'm sure you ladies have much to discuss. You don't need a gentleman about.'

'Nonsense. We will be here for a week. That is plenty of time for us to visit with our aunt.'

'You are staying for the week?' Clara said, her eyes widening as she looked between Lady Juliet and Lady Charlotte.

'It has all been arranged.'

Lady Juliet looked pointedly at Clara and cleared her throat. 'Don't you think Mr Lane should come inside?'

'Of course I do,' Clara said, dropping her niece's hands. 'Won't you join us for some tea?'

'I should be off. I've been here long enough.'

'Then perhaps Mr Lane can join us for dinner tonight?' Her youngest niece was very eager for him to stay. There was no telling if that was good or bad.

'Tonight I am having a musical recital here. Had I known the three of you were coming I would not have arranged it.'

'Is Mr Lane attending?'

Chapter Twenty-Two

Never before had Clara been disappointed to see her nieces. However, once the excitement of knowing that they were back in her home after all this time had subsided, she found she was sad that her day with Lane had been interrupted. She was beginning to realise that he would be leaving Bath soon and that she did not have an infinite amount of time with him.

A deep sense of melancholy washed over her. Her nieces were here—however, part of her wished they had not come. A twinge of guilt hit her as she entered her home and placed Humphrey down on the floor. He scampered off, probably to take a nap, and she notified Darby that she would be serving tea to her nieces.

Walking up the stairs, she recalled the times she had spent in this house with Charlotte, Lizzy, and Juliet. She had no children of her own, but she couldn't have loved these girls any more than if they were her own daughters. She recalled Charlotte running to her here when she received word that her husband had been killed at Waterloo. She could see herself sitting on these stairs, comforting Juliet when she brought her here after the girl's heart had been broken in London.

Charlotte and Juliet arrived in Charlotte's. I followed them in mine.'

'What Lizzy is not saying is that there wasn't enough room for all of us to travel together in her carriage, so I took mine as well. She has too many trunks with her. I honestly don't know how she travelled to Sicily without the ship sinking from the weight of her luggage.'

'I managed to travel lighter than you would believe.'

'And yet here you are at Aunt Clara's for a week with enough luggage to stay for three months.'

'I like to be prepared.'

Juliet was uncharacteristically quiet. Of all her nieces, Clara had spent the most time with Juliet. The girl had lived with her for years here before her recent marriage. Juliet knew her very well. If she needed to fool anyone that she was happy at this moment, it would be Juliet.

Turning to her, she made sure she was smiling. 'And how is married life?'

There was a soft blush that filled Juliet's cheek. 'It is everything I could have wanted.'

Clara reached out and squeezed her hand. 'I knew it would be.' But when she went to remove her hand, the girl held on to it.

'Now tell us about Mr Lane. Does he live in Bath?'

'No. He is visiting.' Once again she was reminded that he was leaving and it became hard to speak.

When the tea tray arrived, she was relieved that arranging the cups on the table and preparing the tea gave her something to do. Unfortunately, it also reminded her of making tea for Lane and how she thought she would be having another cup with him right now.

'You are too quiet.' This time it was Lizzy who spoke.

With her head bent down to fix Juliet a cup of tea, she hoped none of them had noticed.

They had.

At once, Juliet's arm was around her and Lizzy gently reached across the table and took the teacup out of her hand. She refused to look up at them for fear that once she did her tears would begin to flow and she would have a hard time stopping them.

Charlotte took her hand and stroked it in a comforting gesture. 'Talk to us. What has made you so sad?'

The words were stuck in her throat and would not come out.

'Have you been so lonely without me here?' Juliet asked gently. 'I thought the dog might have helped. I've written to you several times a week, but I could write every day.'

'It's not that.'

'Then what is it?'

'Mr Lane will be leaving Bath soon. I know I am all wrong for him. I am too old. But once he leaves I will probably never see him again and I find it hurts my heart.'

'Come now,' Juliet said, 'you are not that much older than he is.'

'But I am old enough. A gentleman his age is thinking about starting a family. A gentleman his age wants to have children. I cannot give him that.'

'Has he talked about wanting children?'

'Well, no. We haven't talked about any of that.'

'Then how do you know that that is what he wants?'

'What man doesn't?'

'I'm sure there are some.'

'Has he given you any indication about what he feels for you?' Lizzy asked with a sympathetic voice.

Chapter Twenty-Three

Lane had planned to take his carriage to Clara's house that night, but after he received a letter from Mr Edwards shortly before he left, he knew a walk would help him work through his anger.

What man turned down an offer to purchase his hotel for that amount of money? It made no sense—and it destroyed Lane's dream of opening a spa here in Bath.

Now he would have to inform Hart, Lyonsdale and Lord Musgrove of it in the morning. It was not something he was eager to do. He took great pride in his business accomplishments. His reputation was built on his ability to consistently find sound and profitable investment opportunities. And while the coffee house would turn a decent profit, it wasn't nearly as large a profit as the spa would have brought. And Lord Musgrove was going to take back news to London that Lane hadn't been able to fulfil his part of the contract.

That cut deep. But as he walked closer and closer to Clara's house, he began to wonder if the pain and anger he was feeling had more to do with knowing that, within the week, he would leave Bath. His time with Clara was coming to an end.

her drawing room. There was a small table with four chairs near the fireplace, where the three Sommersby sisters were deep in conversation, and at the other end of the room were two small sofas that faced one another. Standing around them were the Collingswoods, along with Clara, Mr Greeley and the Dowager. When he took a step further into the room, Harriet took note of him and whispered something into Clara's ear. When their eyes met, it felt as if a soothing balm was placed on his emotional wounds of the day.

Her face brightened and she left her party to approach him. Lane wished with all his heart that he could take her in his arms. He had missed her already and they had only been apart for a few hours.

Clara took him around and reintroduced him to her nieces, each one more welcoming than the next. Greeley appeared relieved to see another gentleman aside from Mr Collingswood in attendance and the Collingswoods were all cordial, but he could sense the mother and father were trying to determine what to make of him and sizing him up against poor Greeley. In all, it wasn't horrible company to be in, but he still would have preferred to be alone with Clara.

It appeared he was the last to arrive and, within a few minutes, the party made its way through a doorway into her dining room. This room was painted the same colour with royal-blue curtains on the tall windows and portraits of men and women from centuries past on the walls. He assumed that some were Clara's ancestors. He searched each face for any resemblance he could see to her. There was a woman in a blue gown with elaborate lace sleeves holding a basket of flowers who looked somewhat like Clara. He could see it in the shape of her brown eyes and that pert upturned nose.

portrait over the fireplace behind Clara. The gentleman in question appeared to be a bit younger than Greeley and was dressed in a scarlet coat with black lapels and a long pale-coloured waistcoat, white breeches and black boots. His cravat had more lace to it than was fashionable now, as was the cut of his coat. He was leaning against a tree, standing beside a horse and looking directly at the viewer with a bemused expression. The position in the room showed the significance of the sitter to Clara.

'That was Uncle Robert,' Lady Charlotte replied in a low voice.

He looked back at her and found her staring at the portrait with a nostalgic smile on her face. 'My grandparents had it painted not long before he married my aunt.'

'He appears to be a genial man.'

It didn't matter how genial the man was, Lane didn't like him.

'Oh, he was. Uncle Robert was our father's youngest brother and very affable. He was one of those lucky people who had the true gift for storytelling. When we were little he would love to tell us these absolutely outrageous tales and as children he would have us all believing them, until he would say this one funny twist at the end of it that let us know it was a Banbury tale.'

'When did he die?'

'I think it's about ten years now.' She picked up her glass of wine and took a sip while appearing to count the years in her head. 'Yes, that's right. Ten years. Time does seem to move at a different pace once you get older, does it not?'

She appeared to be about five years younger than he was, if he had to estimate, and she was right. It was

He didn't want anything to diminish what Clara was feeling for him. Even though he would be leaving her, he wanted to believe that she would miss him for a time and that if his name ever drifted through her mind years from now, it would be accompanied by fond memories.

He was saved from continuing the discussion with Lady Charlotte when the Dowager enquired about the health of her sister-in-law, the Duchess of Winterbourne, and of the work the woman was doing with the Royal Academy. Their discussion gave him the opportunity to turn to his right and steal a glance at Clara, who was sitting next to him at the head of the table.

His heart felt larger when he found her watching him. For how long her eyes had been on him he didn't know, but knowing he had captured her attention somehow made his shoulders go back.

She leaned towards him and lowered her voice. 'I could have placed you beside Mrs Collingswood, but seeing how you and Greeley are of the same rank, I took the liberty of placing you beside me instead of that seat going to her husband, both saving you and me from tedious conversation.'

But he wasn't the same as Greeley and Mr Collingswood, and his prominent place beside the hostess was a sham. Suddenly he was feeling their difference in rank acutely.

'You aren't quietly thinking of dull things to discuss with me, are you?' She gave him a teasing smile. 'If you are, then I assure you that I can think of topics that are duller than yours.'

He leaned closer so their heads were almost touching. 'I doubt that. I have been accused of being as dull as a doornail.'

sat looking at each other while he tried to memorise her with his eyes.

The sound of the Dowager's spoon lightly hitting the inside of her bowl broke the spell between them and they finished their soup course without speaking further.

The remainder of the meal went by pleasantly enough with delicious food and interesting and congenial conversation. As an array of jellies, syllabubs, and fruits were brought to the table, the discussion turned to music.

'Do you remember the last time Lizzy played the harpsichord for us?' Lady Juliet asked, directing her question to Clara.

The Duchess, or Lizzy as her family referred to her, raised her chin. 'Well, I might not have had the patience to practise the harpsichord to play it proficiently, but at least I have a pleasant singing voice.'

Lady Charlotte looked at her sister Juliet. Their exchanged expressions were enough to have the Duchess raise her chin.

'I do. Simon has remarked upon how lovely it is.'

'Simon is in love with you. His opinion does not signify,' Lady Juliet said with a wave of her hand.

'My daughters are accomplished in both singing and playing piano,' Mrs Collingswood said to no one in particular, which made Harriet redden and her sister look down at her lap.

'I, for one, would love to hear them,' Greeley chimed in from his seat beside Harriet. 'My parents had arranged for me to have lessons on our pianoforte so I would be more than happy to accompany them should they choose to sing.' His eyes were on Harriet. 'Or any

Mrs Collingswood's mouth and hand went slack and she almost dropped the spoon that she was holding. Her eyes darted to Clara, who he had yet to look at. He didn't even want to see her out of the corner of his eye. Everyone who was in his line of vision was staring at him. It was obvious that his response was not what any of them expected.

'Why don't we go up to the drawing room now?' Clara said, ending dinner rather abruptly. Her voice was even, but he knew her well enough now that he could hear the suppressed strain in it. 'The harpsichord is in there and you can all decide what it is you would like to perform tonight.'

Juliet was the first one to her feet, followed by the rest of the guests around the table. As if someone else had possessed him, he took a drink of his claret and stood as well. Clara walked behind his chair on her way to the door as was customary for the hostess to lead them out of the room. He was the last one to leave and he looked back at the portrait of her husband and scanned the room that he was certain he would never see again. As he stepped into the parlour, Lady Charlotte, who was walking in front of him, turned and gave him a slight sympathetic smile.

This was how things would end between them. This was how she would remember him. He was the bastard who had sat at her table and pretended to be a gentleman to her and her guests.

The day that he had believed couldn't get any worse suddenly did and he didn't think he was in the mind frame to deal with the consequences. The crushing disappointment that he had felt at not being able to buy the hotel was nothing compared to the pain inside his chest right now. There was no sense in staying and being ig-

Was she going to make him explain it all to her? Did he have to tell her and see the look in her eyes when he did? When he didn't move, she placed her hands on her hips and raised her chin, looking like a warrior preparing for battle.

'You will leave then, before you and I have had a chance to talk about any of this or say our goodbyes… since it appears you are determined to go. I never took you for a man who walked away when life becomes difficult, but it appears I was wrong. If that truly is the type of man you are, then I do believe it is best that you leave. However, I have proper manners and will wish you Godspeed and not simply disappear.'

Her words made his blood run cold. He was not a man who walked away from his problems. He never was and never would be. As she spun around and stormed back to the house, his opportunity to let her know that was slipping away.

'I am not running away,' he insisted, catching up to her before she reached her door.

She stopped in her tracks and turned to him, vexation shone in her eyes. 'Then prove that to be true and talk to me.'

'You have guests. This is not a conversation fit for anyone else's ears but your own. I owe the Collingswoods no explanation of my origins.'

'Then talk to *me*,' she said, poking herself in the chest so hard it had to have hurt. 'Go in that house and talk to me. There are many places we can have a private discussion.'

If it didn't bother her that she was being negligent to her guests and hosting a bastard, then it damned well wasn't going to bother him. 'Fine. After you.' He tossed his hand towards her door and followed her inside.

'Clara, you're the granddaughter of a baron. Your husband was the brother of an earl. I grew up in a Foundling Hospital. Do you know what that makes me? Do you know what that means? I am not just an orphan whose parents have died. I am a bastard—a by-blow of some man who couldn't be bothered to marry my mother. Or was married already when he took her. The only children who are taken in by the Foundling Hospital are bastards. Don't you see? I don't even know on what day I was born or what my real name is—if I was even given one. I am not William Lane. It's the name the Hospital gave me when they took me in. For all I know, my mother didn't even give me a name. For all I know, she never bothered because she couldn't wait to give me away. So, you see, every day my name is a constant reminder that I was discarded and unwanted in the event I ever forget.'

She walked up to him and took his hand into her two delicate ones. The gesture held him in place when in truth he wished he was the type of man to run.

'Is that why you didn't want me to call you William?'

'There is no reason I should have two false names. One is a sufficient enough reminder.'

In her eyes, instead of pity, he saw compassion. Which one was worse he couldn't say, because right now instead of running he wanted to stay with her for ever. And that very thought scared the hell out of him.

When she reached up and slowly ran her fingers through his hair in a comforting gesture, he had to look away. But she guided his jaw gently so he was facing her once more.

'The circumstances of your birth do not change anything. They do not change what kind of man I think you are or the feelings I have for you. I am truly sorry that

on his chest. Without a doubt, she would be able to feel the rapid beating of his heart.

'I will not allow anyone to treat you unkindly in my home. I would just as soon ask them to leave—no matter who it is.'

'I do not need you to champion me, Clara. I am a grown man and have years of experience dealing with people and their prejudices.'

'But I want you to know I will not place you in a position where you have to do that here.'

He cupped her jaw and kissed her one last time before they left the parlour and made their way to her drawing room. She was telling him that she accepted him enough to have him in her home, yet their stations in life were so very different. If he thought he could forget that fact, he was reminded of it in vivid detail when he entered the drawing room with her a few minutes later and the entire room stared at him. Mr Collingswood's dark bushy brows drew together and his wife raised her nose.

'We did not realise how late it was, Mrs Sommersby,' the man said. 'I believe that it is time that we headed home.'

'Thank you for this evening,' his wife added, gathering up her daughters.

Lane walked to the window overlooking the moonlit lawn and could see them bid their farewells to everyone else in the room except for him in the reflection in the glass. Harriet had looked his way a number of times, but was ushered out of the room by her parents. The Collingswoods could go to hell for all he cared—however, the cut still stung and he hated himself for that.

He waited to see who was next to leave the room.

'I had to get married.'

A woman's voice broke the silence and he turned to

didn't want to be dependent on my relatives or become a lady's companion. So, I took all the money I was left with and purchased a hotel. It is what has allowed me to live this comfortable life here in Bath.'

'What?' the Duchess cried in disbelief. 'You're an innkeeper?'

Lady Juliet turned to her sister. 'Why are you so surprised? Surely you knew.'

'No. I did not know. You knew?' Her agitation had not subsided.

'Well, yes, I thought you both knew.'

They both turned to Lady Charlotte, who shook her head. 'I was not aware of this.'

'This is why I never told you. This and the fact that your uncle while he was alive refused to buy one saying it was far beneath our station in life to do so. That if it was known it would affect Juliet's ability to launch well in Society even with a sister who was a duchess. He feared we would lose the friendships of prominent families we knew and the men he went to university with. And he knew your father would have forbidden it. I have kept it quiet to protect you all from any shame it might have caused.'

'I can't believe you're an innkeeper,' the Duchess said again.

The women were talking so quickly it was almost hard to keep track of what they were saying. But the fact that she owned a hotel was stuck front and centre in his mind.

'I'm not an innkeeper, Lizzy. I own The Fountain Head Hotel here in Bath and have someone manage it for me.'

If his brain exploded right now he would not have

discussion going on over by the sofa between the Sommersby women.

'Elizabeth,' the Dowager called out. 'Do you love your aunt any less over this?'

The Duchess sat up and looked between the Dowager and Clara. 'No, of course not.'

'Then pull yourself together. It's not as if she's murdered anyone. She is a woman who, without a husband, has managed to find a way to financial security and she has not had to become a man's mistress to do it. That should be celebrated.'

'It's just so unexpected. That is all.'

'So are many things in life, my dear, but that doesn't mean that they are bad.' She arched her brow at Lane and finished her glass of port. 'Something tells me that you and Mrs Sommersby will have things to talk about tonight. Greeley, I find I am feeling a bit tired all of a sudden. Would you care to walk me home?'

'Of course, Your Grace.'

'It was a pleasure seeing you once more, Mr Lane. I do hope I will see you again soon.' She smiled up at him and patted his arm as she walked past him on her way to say goodnight to Clara and her nieces.

'Goodnight, Mr Lane,' Greeley said, shaking his hand. 'Will you be in Bath for long?'

Now with the knowledge that Clara owned The Fountain Head Hotel, his life had been turned upside down and he didn't know what he would be doing. 'I couldn't say. I was planning on leaving by week's end.'

The man appeared genuinely disappointed. 'Well, I have enjoyed making your acquaintance. If you are ever in town again, please do send your card around. It would be my pleasure to see you again.' He tipped his head one last time and walked across the room.

Chapter Twenty-Four

With the support of her family, it felt as if a giant weight had been lifted off Clara's chest—a weight that she hadn't realised she had been carrying around. She was proud of the business she had built up and she was relieved that she no longer felt as if she had to hide it.

Yet the relief ended the moment she looked across her drawing room to see the unreadable expression on Lane's face. It reminded her how isolated he must have felt growing up without a family. Her heart broke for him because she knew that he had lived in that Hospital without anyone to love and comfort him when he needed it the most. She had been inside that Hospital and seen what it was like. It was where she had met the Dowager while working on a committee to raise funds for it.

When she showed him into her small library that was next to the drawing room, she gestured to him to join her on the sofa and she took a seat.

'I am sorry about the Collingswoods. I am sorry that they made you feel anything less than welcome in my home. You know I do not share their feelings on the matter.'

He sat down next to her and searched her eyes. 'You own The Fountain Head Hotel?'

chased the coffee house a month ago along with a business partner of mine.'

'None of this is making sense. If you own the coffee house, why would you want my hotel as well?'

'Why didn't you accept my offer? It was a very substantial one.'

'Because I do not wish to sell it. And you didn't answer my question.'

'But you could buy another hotel with the money we are offering.' The words came out clipped, taking her aback.

'I don't want the money to purchase another one. That one is doing very well for me.'

He was not being forthcoming with her and it was leaving a prickly sensation running up and down her spine, making her very uneasy.

Suddenly, Lane got up and walked away from the sofa. 'You are being unreasonable,' he declared, pacing the rug in front of her.

That one word enflamed her temper and she stood up as tall as her petite stature would allow. As she planted her hands on her hips, her fingers dug into her skin through her gown. He was not about to accuse her of being unreasonable...or hysterical! 'On the contrary, I am being very reasonable.'

The breath he let out was audible and she could tell he was struggling with what to say.

After all they had shared together, she couldn't understand why he could not explain himself adequately. Marching over to him, she blocked his pacing. 'Talk to me. Tell me why you want my hotel with such fervour. There is something you are not telling me.'

Finally, he met her in the eye and she could see the moment he decided to confide in her. Lane raked his

amount of money to buy it. Clara, you can take that money and invest it in another hotel.'

She didn't want another hotel. There was no guarantee that another hotel would be as successful as this one. She could not take that chance. The fear of losing all her money was still very real for her and the thought of losing her hotel was making her physically sick.

She took his hand in hers. 'I know that this is going to be hard for you to understand, but I cannot sell my hotel. I will not. Too many people are employed there. Those people need their jobs. I will not be responsible for placing them in positions where they will be unable to support themselves or their families.'

'I have no wish to place your staff on the street. I intend to find other jobs for them in the spa.'

'I still cannot sell it to you.'

He removed his hand from hers and rubbed the back of his neck. 'Why? I am giving you a chance to try something new.'

'I don't want to try something new. Don't you see? I am good at making the decisions for *this* hotel. I am good at finding ways to improve the profits that this hotel steadily brings me. It is safe.'

'Safe will not make you rich. Safe will not expand your wealth to a greater degree. You are living very comfortably here, but I am giving you an opportunity to live grander than this.'

'I do not need to live any grander than I am. I have no wish for a country house, or more carriages, or jewels. I am content.'

There was a desperation in his eyes that she couldn't quite understand. He would eventually find another venture to go after. She could not find another Fountain Head Hotel. There was only one.

by chance won a substantial amount of money. I had wanted us to purchase a hotel back here in Bath with it, knowing there was a demand for a quality establishment to cater to the *ton* that gathered here regularly. He saw owning a hotel as beneath our station and refused to consider it each time I brought it up. He decided to invest the money with an old friend from Oxford and lost it all.'

She took a deep breath, recalling the day he arrived at their London town house with the news. She could see how broken he was and how these failures were taking their toll on him.

'The last year of his life, our financial situation became so bad that I lived in fear that we would find ourselves in debtors' prison.' The memories began flooding back and she had to rub her chest to help alleviate some of the squeezing she felt around her heart. 'It's by the grace of God that we did not. After Robert was killed in a riding accident, his older brother discovered the financial state we were in. He was kind enough to settle our debts and provide me with money to secure a new husband—those were his words, not mine. I decided to take that money and instead buy the hotel. And I haven't looked back since.' She leaned closer, needing him to understand. 'That hotel provides me with enough income to live comfortably. That hotel allows me to go to sleep at night and not fear that I will be carted off to prison when I wake up in the morning. You see it as a way to increase your income, but I see it as my protection from the cruel fate that can befall many women in my circumstances. I cannot sell it to you. I'm sorry.'

There was a long pause while he sat forward and rested his forearms on his thighs. He rubbed the thumb of his right hand into the palm of his left and looked

ties into a spa, he wouldn't be leaving Bath for months. She would have more time with him. And if what he told her was true, he was financially sound with his investments. The idea of giving up some of her control was terrifying, but so was the thought of not seeing Lane again.

imagine a kind and loving wife and four sons who he would take fishing and they would give him hugs. He had seen that family perfectly in his mind for many years and he could still picture them today. However, now the kind and loving wife had a face—and it was Clara's. And while that should have felt like such a relief, the reality of it was terrifying.

He had been an unwanted child. What was there to say Clara would want him as a man?

By ten o'clock it was arranged. They'd meet in his office in the coffee house at two. Luckily Lord Musgrove had not yet returned to London and agreed to come to Lane's office for the brief meeting. Since Lyonsdale had just offered to loan them some money to help with the construction, there was no need to include him in this discussion. He would not be involved in the day-to-day responsibilities of running the spa and hopefully soon they would be giving him back the money he'd loaned them with interest.

At ten before the hour, Lane met Clara outside the back door to the coffee house and smuggled her inside, probably in a similar fashion to the way Hart's wife had entered the establishment not long ago. They agreed that he would meet with Hart and Lord Musgrove first and then, when the plan was explained to them, Lane would bring her in. For the time being, she would wait for him in the stockroom opposite his office. It all felt rather clandestine and not at all like the way he was normally accustomed to doing business.

By ten minutes after two, he was sitting behind his desk, trying to convince Lord Musgrove that having

Hart jumped up just in time to move between Lord Musgrove and Lane. 'Perhaps we should take a moment to sit back down and behave like civilised gentlemen.'

'I am a civilised gentleman,' Lord Musgrove spat. 'I don't know what you would call him. This is what I get for trying to do business with a man of no consequence.'

The vein that ran along Lane's temple began to throb and a warm rush of anger heated his face. He went to move around his desk to throttle the man, but once more Hart stepped in the way.

With his back to Lane, he pointed his finger at Lord Musgrove. 'Sir, I will not stand here and allow you to disparage my friend.'

'Well, you won't have to,' Lord Musgrove shouted. 'I am leaving. Our contract stipulates there are three parties involved, not four. It does not include a woman. I will have my secretary contact your solicitor. I am backing out of our contract!'

'You don't need to contact anyone. I'll take care of it for you!' Lane grabbed their contract off his desk and ripped it up.

Lord Musgrove's body stiffened and there was rage in his eyes. He jerked his hat on to his head. 'Barbarian,' he said through his teeth before he stormed to the door and flung it open.

Through the doorway, Lane could see Clara out in the hallway, standing against the wall opposite his door, with a startled expression on her face. Lord Musgrove took one look at her, rolled his eyes at Lane and stormed off to the front door in a huff. Lane would have done anything to go back in time and somehow save Clara from hearing Lord Musgrove's comments.

'Well, that went well,' Hart said, dropping himself into his leather chair and throwing his head back. 'If it

balding man approaching fifty, so this is a pleasant improvement. I understand why you would not want your association known. I will not tell your tale.'

'I am through with hiding this. My nieces are all married now and no longer have a need for me to chaperone them in Society. They have assured me that it is of no consequence to them what people think of their eccentric aunt.'

'The Sommersby sisters are wise women. They take after their aunt—'

'I am sorry,' Lane broke in. 'I had no idea Lord Musgrove would react as he did. Had I known, I wouldn't have suggested any of this to you.'

'Do not blame yourself for other people's actions. This is not your fault.'

From the corner of his eye, Lane could see that Hart was studying them and he recalled how his friend had once fancied Clara.

'Lane informed us you're a shrewd businesswoman, responsible for the success of that hotel. Seeing the reputation it has, I would heartily agree.'

'It was kind of him to say so.'

Hart rubbed his hands together. 'So, we are back in search of a partner. One who has deep pockets and an open mind to investments. Let me talk with Sarah tonight. She might have some ideas.'

'There is no need,' Clara replied, shaking her head. 'I will not be able to go forward with this. I will not sell my hotel or go into any agreement with you gentlemen.'

Instinctively, Lane clasped his hands tighter. 'But we do not have a problem with partnering with you. We will let you make decisions and have a say in what is done.'

'I know you believe that and that might be what hap-

ripped in two. She didn't want him. Once again, he wasn't wanted.

Having to look at the top of her head as she stared at her lap was painful. He wanted to work on trying to forget her as quickly as possible, because he knew it was bound to take him years. However, he was grateful that he was not forced to stand just yet while she walked out on him, because his legs felt too weak to support him.

When she did look up, she swallowed before she spoke. 'Thank you for believing that this could have worked. For giving me the chance to see if this would have been something that I could have wanted. Knowing that you believed in me means more to me than you will ever know.'

He knew why she was walking away from this. He understood what owning that hotel meant to her. He cared for her with every fibre of his being and never wanted her to fear for her future. She deserved peace and security.

'If I had the money and this place was mine, I would create the finest spa Bath has ever seen with you. But I am not the sole owner and I don't have the money on my own to make all of that happen. I wish I did. You don't know how much I wish I did.'

She didn't say anything back. She just nodded.

'I'll be returning to London in a few days. I'm not needed here at the White Bear. Mr Sanderson is competent and trustworthy. He will send me regular reports at the Albany. He doesn't need me looking over his shoulder. I would need another reason to stay.' Their eyes met and he waited. He waited for her to tell him that she wanted him. That she was his reason for staying and that she wanted to have a life with him.

He waited.

'Godspeed, Lane. I will never forget you.' She spun around and rushed out the door, not stopping to close it.

For the first time since he was a child, Lane felt a soul-crushing loss that he knew would take him years to get over.

nieces would be gone in a few days and she knew she would regret it if she didn't spend time with them before they left. It was time to face the world again and doing so surrounded by Charlotte, Lizzy, and Juliet would help ease her pain.

Maria, her maid, was in the best of spirits seeing that her mistress actually wanted to get dressed and might consume more than tea. She had styled Clara's hair with perfect ringlets near her face and suggested her new pink gown which would add colour to her pale complexion. In all, she did a miraculous job hiding Clara's heartache behind a fashionable artifice. At least Clara thought so until she walked into the parlour which was set for breakfast.

All activity at the table stopped and her three nieces stared at her. Humphrey let out a series of excited barks as if to inform them that, yes, their aunt had finally emerged from her solitary confinement and was rejoining Society and they should thank him because it was all his doing. Life was about to go back to the way it was before Mr William Lane appeared in her life.

'You look terrible,' Lizzy said, then shrugged at Charlotte when her sister eyed her sharply.

'I thought Maria had managed very well with my hair today.'

'Your hair is lovely—however, you have dark circles under your eyes.' There was true concern in Lizzy's expression. 'I am worried about you.'

'I haven't been sleeping.'

Juliet held out a chair for her and kissed her cheek when Clara sat down. 'Don't listen to Lizzy, you look beautiful.'

She knew she didn't look anywhere near beautiful and that Lizzy with her honest statements was express-

'No, but you all know about his life. You know that
he has never had a family to love and cherish him the
way we have. Everyone deserves to experience that. Everyone needs that kind of unconditional love. He needs
children. I can never give him that.'

Charlotte placed her hand over Clara's. 'You truly
do love him, don't you?'

'I do. I just want him to find some peace with his
past and be happy.'

'He seemed happy when he was with you.'

The warm tea was comforting, but for the first time
in her life she didn't think she could take another sip.
She pushed the cup and saucer away.

'You've been inside the Foundling Hospital when
you worked on the fundraising committee,' Juliet stated,
eyeing Clara's discarded cup. 'What would it have been
like for him growing up in there?'

'He would have been left there by his mother because
she was unable to keep him. If she intended to return
for him in the future, she would have left a small token
with him that could be used to identify him as her child
since the Hospital changes the children's names.'

'So, his real name is not William Lane?'

She shook her head at Charlotte's question. 'No. He
has no idea what it is or the day of his birth.'

'How very sad. How did they manage to take care
of all the infants in the Hospital? That is a lot of hungry mouths to feed.'

'He would have been given to a wet nurse while he
was an infant and lived with her family in the country until he was five. Then they would have taken him
back to the Hospital where he would live with hundreds
of other children until he reached the age of fifteen.'

'Then would they just release them into London

Chapter Twenty-Seven

Lane had been riding in Hyde Park when he passed a flower border alongside the bridle path of Rotten Row and the scent of roses drifted up on the warm breeze. This was normally his favourite time of year in London. The Season had ended and the streets and parks were less crowded with the carriages of the *ton*, whose members had left town to spend their summer in the country. It was mornings such as this when the sky was clear and the air pleasant that Lane preferred to go for a ride or walk before he would settle in at the desk in his study for a day's work. Today's ride should have put him in good spirits with the ideal weather conditions. But the minute he smelled the scent of roses, his heart constricted in his chest and he cursed himself for deciding on this ride.

Two weeks had passed since he left Bath—two very long weeks. And although he tried daily not to think about Clara, this morning all it took was one whiff of her familiar scent to darken his mood and make him chastise himself for not being able to put the past behind him.

Now he was wondering if the weather in Bath was

Lord Andrew looked up at the building with a nostalgic expression. 'This place was good to me before I settled into married life.' The expression on his face cleared and he looked back down at Lane and adjusted the brim of his hat over his light brown hair. 'Not that I regret a day that I've spent with my wife. Best decision I've made. Tell me, does Brewster still play his violin at five in the morning? I can think of many a day that I wanted to shove the instrument down his throat and I am an early riser.'

'He does and Lord Allum tried to do just that last week. I take it you never told the man about your old neighbour's violin habits.'

Lord Andrew gave a careless shrug. 'It might have slipped my mind.' A flash of humour crossed his face and reached his hazel eyes.

'Convenient for you, not so much for Lord Allum.'

'I suppose you're right.' He shoved both his hands into the pockets of his brown frock coat. 'Give my best to Roberts and Jeremy,' he said, regarding two of the porters. 'It was good to see you again, Lane.' With that he tipped his head, turned and strolled back towards Piccadilly.

As he entered the building, Lane's curiosity got the better of him and he shook the parcel as he made his way down the corridor to his set of rooms. Nothing shifted. Nothing rattled. He turned it over in his hand and once again puzzled over the unknown handwriting.

After unlocking his door, he was greeted by Burrows, his butler, who took his hat and gloves and went to see about arranging coffee for Lane. Since the day was warm, he slipped out of his green-linen frock coat and tossed it over the chair beside the sofa in his par-

the etching. His finger stilled when he read the line of script.

William

His heart started racing and he flipped it over, but there was nothing on the other side. The denomination had been rubbed off and it was just a smooth, plain surface with a few scratch marks on it. He turned it over in his palm so his name appeared face up once again.

Hope started to blossom that it might be from Clara—that maybe, just maybe, she still thought about him. She had told him once that she would miss him. Maybe after all this time she still did and this was her way of letting him know.

With his one hand, he flicked open the folded paper he had placed on his lap and scanned the handwritten contents to find the name scratched at the bottom. It was Clara.

His heart skipped a beat and for the first time in his life he had to clear his vision to read his correspondence.

Dear Lane,
I hope with all my heart that this letter finds you well. I realise I am taking the risk that this might never reach you, but it is a risk I must take since I am not able to deliver this to you in person.

Lord Andrew Pearce is Charlotte's husband and he has informed her that he is an acquaintance of yours. Knowing him to be a man of honour, I am certain that he will deliver this to you unopened.

You once told me that the one thing you wished for most in the world was to know if your mother

Chapter Twenty-Eight

June was Clara's favourite month. The weather was warmer, her favourite roses were in bloom and the days were longer. Except this year, she would have preferred shorter days so she could have spent more time in bed, asleep. It was only while she was sleeping that she didn't feel the daily pain of missing Lane. Aside from being with Humphrey, tending to her roses was the only bit of joy she could find lately.

On this particular morning, she had spent time in her garden cutting roses with Juliet, who was in town with her husband looking for a house to buy. Now that her niece had left, she was arranging a bunch of pink and yellow roses in a green Sèvres vase that rested on the harpsichord in her drawing room when Humphrey attempted to gnaw on the leg of the instrument.

'Humphrey, no.' She used her firmest voice and he stopped what he was doing and looked up at her with his big dark eyes. 'You have already destroyed my favourite slippers. You will not be attacking my furniture as well. Go play with your bone.'

Humphrey tilted his head, his black ears flopping with the movement, and looked back to where she was

lick his hand before he gave the dog a final pat on the head and stood up and adjusted the cuffs of his navy-linen coat. Humphrey let out a series of happy barks as he took a few steps back. All the while his tail continued to swish from side to side and, like Clara, his attention did not waver from the man in front of him.

They stood twenty feet apart and it was as if neither of them wanted to take a step forward for fear of breaking this perfect moment. Slowly he walked towards her and the highly polished leather of his black boots shone in the sunlight. Clara had to blink a few times to make certain she wasn't imagining things.

He stopped about a foot away from her and seemed to study her as if he was savouring this moment of seeing her once more. She didn't think they would ever be in the same room together again. She didn't think if he ever came back to Bath that he would seek her out. The shock of being this close to him ran through her body and she placed her hand over her ribs in the hopes of steadying her heart that was thundering in her chest.

'I don't even know how to begin thanking you for what you did for me.'

The token. Of course, that was why he was here. It had nothing to do with his feelings about her. He knew she was all wrong for him. For all she knew he had already found some woman to replace her—someone younger.

'How did you get in here?'

'Lady Juliet let me in. She was leaving your home just as I was about to knock. She told me that there was a chance you would not agree to see me and that she thought it was important that I did.'

It was impossible to take a deep breath even though she was trying.

sofa. Even though he was raised as an orphan, he possessed exceptional manners and waited until she was seated before he sat down beside her.

'I have to ask, how were you able to find it? How did you even know it existed?'

She fiddled with the white muslin of her dress that covered her knee because it was becoming too painful to look at him. 'I didn't know for certain, but I knew there was a chance your mother had left something with you.'

There was an intensity in his expression when she looked up at him, as if he were paying close attention to every syllable she uttered. 'Years ago, I had been on a fundraising committee at the Hospital. I'd been through the building a number of times and know the procedure for how the children are taken in. I was shown tokens that were left with some of the children who had been admitted that week. Not all look like yours. I've seen scraps of cloth and single playing cards. All sorts of things, really. And not every mother leaves something. I only hoped that your mother had.'

'But I don't understand. How did you even find it? How do you know it's mine?'

'I knew the year of your birth. The information that was taken when you were admitted was sealed in a billet with that token and your new name. It took some time going through all the billets for 1782 and 1783.'

'I was told that information about me would never be released.'

'It's not supposed to be.' She looked away, embarrassed to admit the next bit. 'We might have circumvented the rules.'

For the first time since he arrived a hint of a smile was on his face. 'We?'

She was done hiding things from the people she cared about. And it was better that he knew this about her in the event her gift to him had him considering that they had a future together.

'I came to help the Foundling Hospital because I could not have any children of my own. You see, I never was able to carry a child to its birth. My womb has some kind of defect. That is why I never had any children.'

He stilled and, even though he was looking at her, Clara didn't think he saw her.

'Is that why you took the waters in Bath?'

She swallowed before nodding slowly. 'I was advised the waters might strengthen my body. It never did work, but it became a bit of a habit, I suppose. I don't do it now for that reason, of course. Now it just helps with the occasional ache or two.'

'I'm sorry. That must not have been easy for you.'

A sympathetic expression showed in his eyes that touched her heart and she had to look away.

'It wasn't easy, but in time both Robert and I came to accept it. I wasn't able to give the Hospital any funds. We frequently didn't have any to spare. However, being able to help those children in any way I could somehow helped my soul heal from the loss of not having a child.'

'So, you truly do understand where I come from. That night when I admitted it at the table and we talked afterwards, you knew I was a by-blow before I even informed you of it.'

'I did and told you that it did not change how I felt about you. I doubt anything could.'

'Felt...you no longer feel the same way about me?'

'That night feels like a lifetime ago.'

'And now?'

He was asking her to explain her feelings to him.

'Don't what?'

'Letting you go is hard enough. Don't make it worse.'

'Then don't let me go.'

When she opened her eyes, he saw pain there. 'We have no future together. It is better if we don't prolong this.'

'You don't want a future with me?'

'I didn't say that.'

'Then what are you saying?'

'I'm saying you deserve more in life than I can give you.' There was a catch in her voice.

'You are what I want in my life. You are the only thing.'

'You say that now and maybe you mean it, but you will not feel that way ten years from now. You deserve to have that family that you were denied years ago. I cannot give that to you.' There was a pleading sound in her voice as she turned away from him. She was asking him to end this conversation and she might even be wanting him to leave.

He wasn't going anywhere.

'All I want is you.' He placed his hand gently on her clasped hands when what he really wanted to do was hold her tightly and not let her go. 'Clara, look at me... Clara.'

She turned with tears streaming down her beautiful face. His heart twisted a bit more as he placed soft kisses on her eyelids in an attempt to stop her tears.

'You are all the family I need. I have never had a father and have no idea how to be one. While I have thought of having children, I cannot miss anything that I have not had. I cannot miss children that do not exist. We don't need children to be a family, Clara. You and I are all the family I could ever want.'

tongue against hers, she tangled her fingers through his hair and gave a gentle tug.

He wanted to possess her completely. His hands moved to her breasts, confined in her stays and in her soft cotton gown. The passionate need inside him was growing. He needed to touch her bare skin and broke the kiss to trail his lips down the column of her neck. She smelled faintly of roses and it had become his favourite scent.

She was working at the knot of his cravat and her breathing was becoming laboured.

'I want you,' he said into her collarbone, licking her skin and gently squeezing her full round breasts. 'I want to be with you more than anything.'

His cravat was tossed to the floor and she worked his coat over his shoulders. 'I want that, too,' she replied, breathlessly tilting her head to give him better access to the base of her neck.

She clung to him as he laid her down and trailed his hand up her leg. His desire for her was overriding everything else as he skimmed his fingers up the soft skin of her thigh until he couldn't go any further and he sank his fingers into her warmth. He could feel her work the buttons of the fall of his breeches as she periodically arched her back as he moved his hand faster.

When she climaxed with a soft cry, he was aching for her. He was aching to fill her and claim her as his own. Her delicate hand encircled his length with a firm grip and slid up and down.

'I want this. I want you,' she said in between kisses.

And as he slid himself inside her for the first time, she grasped his forearms while they watched each other intently with their foreheads touching. It didn't take long before they found a rhythm all their own through

you marry me. I will do anything for you not to fear for your future again. And I meant that you are everything in this world that I need. I don't need your hotel. I need you and want to spend the rest of my life with you in my arms. I want to marry you, Clara, if you'll have me.'

There was a catch to her breath and she brought her hand up to her lips. 'You mean that, don't you? You truly do.' In her eyes, he saw it. He saw that she knew for certain there was no hesitation on his part. She knew he was earnest in his proposal.

'I will marry you, William. I will.'

He hadn't had anyone call him by that name in years. The sound of it on her lips touched a part of him that he didn't even know existed. His heart was ready to burst. And more than anything he was grateful that he had found her and that she would be calling him that every day for the rest of their lives.

her skirt and up the back of her leg. The sensation sent a delicious shiver to her most intimate places.

'I thought you said you needed my help with inventory since Mr Sanderson is visiting his sick mother.'

'I did. We are finished and I thought I'd show you my appreciation.'

'We are in the storeroom.'

'That never stopped us before,' he offered with a lift of his brow.

His hand travelled up over her knee and Clara had to hold on to his shoulders to steady herself. A small satisfied smile lifted the corner of his mouth. Just as his hand begin to skim up her thigh, there was a knock on the door behind him. His hand froze.

'Yes,' he called out, not breaking their gaze.

'There is someone here to see you, sir,' Hatchard replied through the door. The young man who they had hired from the Foundling Hospital was settling in nicely, assisting Mr Sanderson here in the coffee house.

The disappointment on William's face was obvious as he removed his hand from Clara's thigh and helped her down from the chair.

'Did you have an appointment?' she asked, shaking out her skirt.

'No.'

He opened the door and startled the slight, dark-haired young man who immediately averted his eyes. Did all of their employees assume when they were spending time in the storeroom that they weren't exactly working? She had only been in that room four times with him.

'Do you know who it is, Hatchard?'

'Yes, sir, it's the Dowager Duchess of Lyonsdale.' From the expression on his face when he said Eleanor's

I will not think you rude.' She kissed his cheek for good measure.

'Very well. I will take my paperwork from the stables and head home. I can work at my desk in our parlour just as easily as I can here.'

When he opened the door, they found Eleanor standing by the window, looking outside. She turned with a smile when she saw them.

'You have been spending quite a bit of time here this week and I wasn't far so I thought I would see if you were here first before I went to your home.'

'Please, have a seat,' Clara said, gesturing to the pair of chairs in front of William's desk. She knew that look in Eleanor's eyes. Some exciting bit of gossip was about to make the rounds of Bath.

'Do you recall the other night you said the Collingswoods had been particularly quiet and you thought they might have returned to London without saying goodbye?'

Clara and William exchanged glances. Now they would find out why the house next door had been dark for the past week. Eleanor always seemed to find out things other people could not.

'Well,' she continued, sitting on the edge of her chair, 'I received a letter from Greeley today. He was writing to thank me for introducing him to Miss Collingswood. It seems that your Harriet had been introduced to another man while you were on your honeymoon and Greeley was away working on Lyonsdale House. This gentleman had just become a baron and showed interest in Harriet. Her parents had favoured the match and were actively attempting to keep Harriet and Greeley apart.'

'That's terrible! Why did Harriet not write to me in Paris and tell me this?'

and there by the way you looked at one another. Why do you think I left you alone during that ball in the Assembly Room? Why do you think I barely spoke to you during the performance of Mr Sheridan's play? I know a love match when I see one.'

Clara wasn't certain she would give Eleanor credit for bringing her and William together. She liked to think that fate had something to do with it that day at the Pump Room. If he had arrived an hour earlier or if she had chosen to stay home that day, they would never have spoken. And when her dress had got caught in the shrubbery in the park, fate had chosen that path for him to take that day.

She had a lot to thank the heavens for. But the one thing she was grateful for more than anything else was that she had been given a second chance to find love in her life. And she could not have asked for a better man to share this part of her life with.

Their voices must have woken Humphrey, who had been sleeping under Clara's chair. He lifted himself with a yawn and slowly padded over to the other side of the desk. She could tell by his languid movements that he wasn't finished with his nap yet and Clara knew that right now he was resting his head on William's booted foot. There was a special bond between that dog and her husband and she would bet good money that William would not be reviewing his reports from the stable at home. He never would disturb their dog while he fell asleep on him. She wondered if he ever marvelled at how much his life had changed in such a short amount of time all because of the water here in Bath.

* * * * *

Historical Note

The Foundling Hospital, where Lane grew up, was the first children's charity in the UK. It was established in 1739 by philanthropist Thomas Coram to help care for and educate children who had been abandoned by their parents due to severe poverty or illegitimacy. Joining him in this venture were the artist William Hogarth and the composer George Frideric Handel.

Later, admission to the Foundling Hospital became restricted to the first children of women of good character whom the father of the child had deserted. In placing her child with the Hospital, the unmarried mother would be able to earn an honest livelihood.

By the time the Foundling Hospital closed, in 1954, it had taken care of approximately twenty-five thousand children.

To find out more information about this important part of London's history and the tokens that were left with some of the children, visit my website at *www.lauriebenson.net* and search my blog. You can also visit the Foundling Hospital museum, as well as browse their website.